THE RUN-OUT

Robert Crampsey

THE
RUN-OUT

Robert Crampsey.

Richard Drew Publishing
Glasgow

First published 1985 by
Richard Drew Publishing Ltd
6 Clairmont Gardens, Glasgow G3 7LW
Scotland

Crampsey, Robert A.
The run-out
I. Title
823'.914[F]   PR6053.R3/

ISBN 0-86267-097-7

Typeset by John Swain (Glasgow) Limited
Printed in Great Britain by
Butler & Tanner Ltd, Frome and London

CONTENTS

'Either batsman shall be out, RUN OUT, if in running or at any time while the ball is in play . . . he is out of his ground and his wicket is put down by the opposite side . . . If the batsmen have crossed in running, he who runs for the wicket which is put down shall be out; if they have not crossed, he who has left the wicket which is put down shall be out. If a batsman remains in his ground, or returns to his ground, and the other batsman joins him there, the latter shall be out if his wicket is put down.'

Laws of Cricket, 37.1, 37.3

'At ten minutes to five yesterday afternoon at Westercote, Glamorgan looked bound for defeat and the prospects of a new name on the championship roll of honour were bright. The home side, set to get 188 in 95 minutes plus twenty overs, were strongly placed at 106 for 3. Then Applegarth, 66 not out and looking in no difficulty, played a controlled drive to Llewellyn at deepish mid-off, the safest of singles. He arrived at the other end to find that, inexplicably, Palfreyman was contemplating the view. The veteran hurled himself towards home but, although the throw was a trifle wayward, Eifion Jones was equal to the occasion and Applegarth was out — narrowly. Disintegration followed and within forty minutes the innings had subsided at 157 all out. There are reports of stirring dressing-room scenes.'

Daily Telegraph

The Incident

As the bowler went back to his mark at a resigned amble, Frank Applegarth had a quick look at the sky. Cloud was building up from the west but, with twenty years' experience of this ground, he reckoned that they were good for two hours yet before any real prospect of rain, and long before that this match would be determined.

The bowler had halted by the umpire and was drawing the latter's attention to the shape of the ball, or rather its mis-shape. The batsman watched him sourly. Go ahead, mate, he thought, it'll not affect me one iota. When we win this we've closed to within six points of Middlesex, and I'd rather take Warwick here and Worcester away than Northants and Essex at Lords with a trip to Scarborough thrown in. That'll tax John Michael's undoubted gifts of captaincy.

The square leg umpire had wandered in for the reverential discussion of the ball which marked these occasions. He shook his head and tossed it back to the bowler, with an invitation to get on with it. The local radio commentator murmured breathily to his microphone, 'Ezra Moseley, then, this tall Barbadian, to bowl to Applegarth from the

Crippledyke End, 106 for 3, 188 to get, about seventy minutes to go.'

The Barbadian ran smoothly and speedily to the wicket, his arm circled, and the ball pitched on off stump. Applegarth had noticed, rather to his surprise, that Mike Llewellyn had been dropped back by his skipper to a fairly deep mid-off. Strange; in Malcolm Nash's position, he thought, he'd have been crowding the batsman, only chance really with a mere eighty odd left to get and seven wickets with which to get them. Ours not to reason why, my son. Down came the bat in the controlled off-drive which would take the ball slowly to mid-off in the safest of singles. As he made contact with the ball, he snapped, clearly and without stress, 'Come one,' and set off at a comfortable pace for the non-striker's end. A free gift, this single, and on a day when he was in form anyway.

It was perhaps because it was such an obvious single that he had got to the other end before he realised that Richard Palfreyman had not moved. Within touching distance of him, he heard the youngster say something quite clearly. Typically, Applegarth tried to get back, and almost made it. The fielder had very naturally conceded the single and had moved to the ball at no great pace. Consequently his throw as Applegarth hurled himself into despairing, lung-searing reverse, lacked its normal precision, and Eifion Jones had to take the ball high and wide of the stumps. Even so, his gauntleted hand swept the bails off a good two yards before Applegarth slid a hopeless bat into the crease. The batsman's look to the umpire was that of the wretch to the hanging judge. He needed no confirmation, and was off in a heavy, doom-laden silence which lasted until he was almost at the edge of the small wooden pavilion, when the members gave him the reception his 66 deserved. The little scoreboard got it right immediately — the main one always needed five minutes and a telephone call to adjust to any major — indeed minor — change.

Applegarth, lips compressed, walked between the rows of members, the 'Well played, Frank's' and 'Bad luck, Frank's' coming with all the greater warmth because the match could surely still be won, and with the winning of it would be the probability of the championship. The County had never managed that in all its history. It was a small county, short on population and large towns, but of recent years counties as small had flown the championship pennant. There had been success in the one-day competitions, which pleased most of the members and delighted Eric Constable, the Treasurer, but until the championship was won, the County would always be regarded as inferior, unfulfilled.

As the game tilted swiftly and irrevocably towards Glamorgan, Applegarth sat in the empty dressing-room, occasionally brushing his sweat-streaked face with an elbow, still padded-up, the groans of the members an all too accurate intelligence system. The skipper, Peter Latimer, went to a brilliant bat/pad catch at short leg, there was an equally brilliant run out and an lbw decision for a ball that was straight but high. Palfreyman hung around for 27 and the West Indian paceman, Rupert Delaval, hit a bright 15 which never offered permanence, but Glamorgan took the game by the throat. With the total at 157 the last pair came back to the pavilion, the Welshmen pushing Moseley ahead to take the plaudits with his 4-47, and the members managing to bring their hands together despite their numbing disappointment. By that time the little terrace in front of the pavilion was astir with the report that on his return to the dressing-room, Richard Palfreyman had been felled by a blow from his senior colleague.

11

CHAPTER 1

The Striker

When people told him that 'he played cricket like a Yorkshireman', Frank Applegarth simply grunted in the unprepossessing way he had. He would have dearly loved to be a Yorkshireman, indeed, born in Thornton Curtis in North Lincolnshire, he had missed that happy distinction by less than five miles, but it might as well have been five thousand. A Thornton Curtis lad could no more play for Yorkshire than an urchin from the streets of Katmandu. Lord Hawke had decreed as much, although Applegarth seemed to remember someone telling him that the noble lord was himself a Lincolnshire man.

Well, if so, that was something they had in common, about the only thing. He'd looked Lord Hawke up in *Wisden* one time — Eton, Cambridge, Yorkshire, President of MCC. With a background like that you could hardly fail, a bit different from Thornton Curtis village school and then the secondary modern in Cleethorpes when his father moved into the town.

Of all the things that annoyed and disappointed Alice Applegarth about her husband, his tendency at times to be 'poor-mouth' ranked very high. The truth was that, from an admittedly unpromising background, there had been hardly a rock on his path to success in the first-class game. In 1960, when he was seventeen, his club had come south on tour, and in a match in the county town he had scored a sparkling eighty in jig time, enhancing his performance by three catches behind the wicket and a stumping.

The County was then going through the worst period of its history, four times in the last five years it had propped up the championship table. He had been invited down for coaching the following Easter, taken on the staff almost immediately, and here he now was in his twenty-first season with them. He had spent a season and a bit in the seconds, where they moved him from number six to second wicket down, and told him to forget his wicket-keeping, since in taking the off-spinner his initial, instinctive movement was back. Then in 1962 he came in for the third match of the summer against Northants at Kettering, scored 18 in his first innings and 41 in the second, and had never looked back.

The many milestones had been passed — sixteen times he'd got his thousand plus for the season, five times he'd reached two thousand. After four years he'd got his first cap against New Zealand, and while never making himself a permanency in the England side, he tended to be recalled whenever the selectors were in bother for the less glamorous tours, so that the bulk of his Test experience had been acquired against the Kiwis, Pakistan and India.

He had done pretty well from his benefit in 1973, and there was a testimonial the season after next, when he looked to get near the £23,000 which his benefit had brought in. He'd learned a few things from the earlier occasion, the importance of stomping the County and attending all events, however uncongenial — the Fashion Show, the Sports Quiz, the Darts Match. He lacked the verbal dexterity to be at ease on such occasions, and his team-mates resented the habit by which he appropriated their witticisms and retailed them as his own. He could have done, he thought, with Peter Latimer's effortless command of English and knack of delivering exactly the right couple of sentences. Nature's law of compensation maybe, the skipper could certainly have used *his* square-cut or on-drive.

A fair living then, if only in the last ten years, a Gillette medal, a John Player success, and thirty-thousand runs — thirty-one, he corrected himself — as a career aggregate, and until today a very possible shout of a championship, to say nothing of the chance of nine centuries in a season, something no one had ever achieved with the County. In mid-August he, Applegarth, had eight, today he was on 66 not out, not in any vestige of difficulty, until that malevolent young bastard Palfreyman . . .

Still out there he was, bloody strokeless wonder, grubbing around, meat and drink for the Taffs, if they were allowed to set a close field.

The door opened, and a bat hurtled towards the corner of the miniscule dressing-room, in which it seemed a physical impossibility that eleven grown men could change. The squat figure of Bernie Masterton, wicket-keeper and occasional forcing bat, made its cursing entrance. Even in his morose fury, Applegarth noted the keeper's bulging gut with disdain. His team-mate was agile enough, but cricketers had an obligation to look like athletes. Those who didn't, gave ammunition to the 'over-paid, under-trained beerswillers' lobby.

The fat man hurled his gloves to join his bat and removed his pads in a stream of monotonous obscenities.

Applegarth put his own problems behind him momentarily.

'Where are we at, Bernie?'

'One hundred and thirty-fucking-seven for seven.'

'What happened?'

'Malcolm bowled me one, dead straight but skyscraper high. He asked politely, as much for a laugh as anything, and that stupid bastard Dodd stuck his finger up.'

'You reckon it was over the top then?'

Masterton plucked at his shirt. 'Over the top? There'll be a bruise on my right tit.'

'Not the greatest is Dodd. I thought I'd made it.'

'Aye, it was a close one,' said the keeper without conviction, as, delving into his flannels, he fished out his box.

'You looked pretty set, Frank,' he grunted, removing his boot with a heave.

'I could've played the buggers with a toothbrush.'

'What went wrong, didn't you call?'

'Of course I called.'

'Did he send you back?'

'No.'

'Did he hear you, d'you think?'

'Of course he heard me.' Applegarth underlined his conviction by a staccato burst of swearing.

'Then, for Christ's sake, what was young Richard at?'

'He ran me out, quite deliberately,' Applegarth said in an expressionless mutter.

'Oh, come off it, Frank.'

'He ran me out, Bernie,' Applegarth repeated in the same flat, considered tone.

'He ran you out, of course, we all saw that. But not deliberately. Why the hell would he do that?'

'I intend to ask him.'

16

'Look, Frank,' Bernie said uneasily, 'draw it mild, eh? We all get uptight about these things, especially when we're so near the pennant. But what you've said is the most serious thing you could say about a professional cricketer, any cricketer, come to that.'

'That's right.'

The keeper looked at him curiously, towel round his bare shoulders, another one in his hands. There was a shout from outside. Masterton jumped up on the bench and peered out of the window.

'Aye, aye! Your man's gone! Eifion got him one way or another, they're backslapping away at him.' He got up heavily. 'Shower, here I come. Not this year, Frank. Going outside to watch the last rites eh?'

'No. Even rain's no good to us now.'

'You don't think Rupert and Sammy can make 57 for the last wicket?'

'That's right. The shower's that way.'

The wicket-keeper looked obliquely at his team-mate but said nothing as he departed, wearing a jockstrap and clutching soap and towel, for the rusty, inadequate shower. A few minutes later he was conscious of raised voices and a crashing of tables from the dressing-room. Hastily emerging from the tepid spray, he pushed the door open in time to see Richard Palfreyman reel to the floor, to be followed down by Applegarth. It took the combined efforts of Masterton, a committee-man and the captain to drag Applegarth off.

The cramped dressing-room was a bedlam of voices, seeking explanations, making denunciations, shouting for medical help. It was quite five minutes before Palfreyman finally came round. Jack Winant, the club doctor, said he would run him to the Alexandra for X-ray, just in case.

Before he could do so, the last two batsmen were pushing through the narrow door, having fallen thirty-one runs short of their target.

Palfreyman was evacuated, the captain sent for the President, and there was a brief exchange with Applegarth. He was asked to report early to the ground the following morning, when a fuller investigation would be held. In the meantime, he was reminded of that section of his contract which prevented him from making any unauthorised statements to the Press. He was further reminded that, whereas the County had taken a generous view of an earlier breach after a match at Trent Bridge three seasons ago, he could look for no such indulgence should there be any repetition.

To all of this he responded with curt nod and monosyllable, enlarging this to 'I've nothing to say' to the two hopeful cricket writers who flanked him on his way across the field to his car. He vaulted the low stone wall which enclosed the ground and opened the door of his Cavalier, which in large letters proclaimed that it was a gift to Frank Applegarth, for the use thereof, from David Haxton and Son, Contractors, St Mary Pole. He switched on the ignition, and used the windscreen-washer to wipe away the accumulation of fallen leaves and dead insects. As the windscreen cleared he became aware of the little spots, isolated, growing in number. The rain had arrived, and it would be all of four days before it moved away.

CHAPTER 2

The County Captain

Peter Martin Latimer was in his third season as County skipper, and the fracas between Applegarth and Richard Palfreyman was the first major disruptive incident that had occurred in that time. He was not at all sure how it ought to be dealt with, although it had already been decided who would deal with it. The matter would be handled in the first place by three men, the President, the Chairman of the cricket committee, and himself.

He was not looking forward to the investigation, or the hearing, whichever you cared to call it. Blame would have to be apportioned, with the strong possibility of permanently alienating one or other player. He sighed, and having vainly tried to stretch his six foot two inches in the bath, made as comfortable a curl as possible in the hot water.

He had seen the incident, that was fortunate, had seen it clearly. He was on his way back to the pavilion from the caravan which served as the Secretary's office during Westercote week, and although not absolutely dead in line with the crease, he was well enough placed to be quite sure that Applegarth was out. He was also quite sure that it was a perfectly good call of Frank's for the single — in the old pro's phrase, 'there was one and a half there.' The old boy was on song, batting with the remorseless efficiency that was his trade-mark. Whoever was to blame for the run out, it wasn't he, and no matter how criminally stupid the loss of the wicket, the game should still have been won. It had slipped away, and so too had the Championship. Not mathematically, that was still on, but Latimer refused to delude himself with calculations that they would take maximum bonus points from the remaining two games — and win them — while Middlesex would lose all three remaining matches. No, it was gone, and second was the best the County could do.

He reached out a long, abstracted arm and soaped himself thoughtfully. Second was no bad position for the County, unprecedented if you cared to be pedantic about it, two third places in one hundred and three years had been the height of achievement in the county championship. He knew intuitively that had they won today, they could have blocked out Middlesex, especially if John Michael were away on Test duty for two of their last three fixtures. And one daft mistake! Still, young players were entitled to make mistakes, and Applegarth's reaction had been in every sense intolerable.

It was six years since the name P.M. Latimer had first appeared on the County team sheet, on this very ground, the season before he captained the 'Varsity. In the Lord's match that year he had done well with two gritty forties, and he was pleased to be asked to play for his native county. His thought was that he might have the remainder of that summer and the next on the county circuit, if he could hold his place, before settling down to a career as a Classics master, if he could find a school which still taught the subject.

He well remembered that Applegarth had not been exactly effusive in his welcome, had indeed been barely civil. Later, when relations improved, after the bust-up when Latimer was first made captain, he christened his dour team-mate 'Hard-times' Applegarth, a label which the recipient wore with a certain grim relish.

The young undergraduate had felt very much on trial. Applegarth was prone to making vaguely-directed remarks just within hearing about 'fancy-caps' who decided to play a little cricket in August, when the hard work had been done. Latimer grinned at the memory as he stood up in the bath. 'Fancy-caps' — the archaic word tickled him, there hadn't been one of the breed for the past twenty years or more.

He'd gone back up to University as captain the following season, and again returned for the last six weeks to the County. He seldom failed, he equally seldom made a lot of runs, but he was good for thirty-odd most days, got by pushes and nudging deflections. His off-spinners turned sharply, if erratically, and his work in the field, whether at cover or gully, was outstanding. On Sundays, pushed back to deep point on the fence, his speed — despite his height — and the accuracy of his throwing meant that he was normally fifteen to twenty runs in credit before he came to the wicket. He lost his awe of the great men as he discovered that Test bowlers could be hit, and Test batsmen could, occasionally, be bowled.

Even so, he was surprised at the end of that summer in which he came down, to be offered a contract with the County for the following season. Even better, it appeared that it would be possible for him to teach the autumn and spring terms at Marlborough, though he would be expected to help with the hockey, since he was a double Blue.

He had often since reflected how fortunate he was to have come into cricket in the mid-1970s when sponsorship and the proliferation of competitions made it possible to knock out a half-decent living from the game, a very good one for those who achieved Test status. Ten years earlier he would simply not have been able to make the financial sacrifice, now he was being adequately paid for something he loved doing.

He had two seasons of wary neutrality with Applegarth until, just three years ago, Paul Day, the then captain, had fallen out with the committee over selection policy and taken himself off to Hampshire. In quick succession Frank Applegarth and Latimer had been called before the committee, the first to be told that he was not to be the new captain, and the second to be offered the job.

It was a peculiarity of the County that the position of President carried executive rather than merely prestigious status. There had been rumblings from a section of the membership about this, but so far the constitution had withstood all threats of revision. The news of the appointment was therefore conveyed to Latimer by the President, Brigadier General Sir Anthony Coverdale.

'We've decided to ask you to skipper the side next season, Latimer. Take over for the last two games and don't worry how we do. The job's yours next summer if you want it.'

Delighted and embarrassed, Latimer sought to know why the choice had fallen on him.

'Have you considered the position of Applegarth, Sir Anthony?' he enquired. 'As senior man he might reasonably have expected to have been asked to take over. And he's certainly the best cricketer in the side.'

'He is, of course,' said the Brigadier smoothly, 'which

ironically is one of the reasons for wanting you. As long as he's with us, Applegarth will be in the England team or on the fringe of it. Put it another way, he'd be away for roughly half the county matches in any one season. Someone else would have to step in anyway. Besides you've a season's captaincy with the 'Varsity under your belt and we don't feel that old Frank has any particular tactical aptitude. Take the job like a good chap.'

Even then, he had asked for time to consider. He well knew his limitations as a player, and the shores of county cricket over the last twenty years were strewn with the wrecks of amateur captains whose sides had given them a hard time — Tom Pugh of Gloucestershire, Peter Kirby of Leicester, Jackie Blackledge of Lancashire. Even Ronnie Burnett had suffered considerably before coming good in his second season with Yorkshire. It was true that he himself would be paid for playing, but in every other aspect the situation seemed dauntingly similar to the instances cited.

He deliberated overnight and said that he would assume the captaincy. Initially Applegarth and Bernie Masterton made life hard for him. The star batsman offered no major overt criticism, but with thick blond eyebrows would signal eloquently his opinion of field placings. His first team talks were received in a silence which was non-involved rather than respectful. And his batting, at that time always just a shade the right side of moderate, suffered under the responsibility of captaincy. He was, however, sustained by the unwavering support of the President and the cricket committee.

In the June of his first full season, he had a cherished belief confirmed. He *was* a better captain than Applegarth. The latter had taken over the side for two games when Latimer was out with a bruised thumb caused by a Jackman lifter at Guildford. He had the chance to observe his rival and was able, quite objectively, to categorise his leadership as leaden and over-cautious. His handling of the bowlers was orthodox in the extreme, he was reluctant to use spinners, and when he did the first four hit off them brought an anxious look and the second a bowling change. He had no clearly thought-out alternative batting order, and his declarations were so cautious as to be insulting.

The first game of Latimer's return gave him his chance. He put down a sharp but takeable chance in the gully off Kirsten at Buxton, to the audible disgust of Applegarth at second slip. The missed chance cost ninety runs and would have cost the match had he and Rupert Delaval not hung around for nearly two hours while putting on seventy-eight runs for the ninth wicket. That evening he asked Frank Applegarth to come to his room in the hotel.

'Cards on the table, Frank, it's about your attitude to me as skipper. I don't like it, I want it changed. I know you may well feel the job should have gone to you.'

'That's not for me to say,' the other said dourly.

Latimer smiled. 'Exactly right, Frank. It's not for you to say. It's for the county committee to say, and they gave the job to me. I'd rather have arrived at an accommodation pleasantly, but the time for that is well gone. So, here it is. I'm skipper, you're not. You can work with me, or against me, your good influence on the side could be enormous. I need your help. I'd greatly value it. I've some right to expect it. If I get it, well and good. If not, I'll run the side my way, and if you obstruct me I shan't hesitate to drop you.'

It was a courageous bluff — the committee might back Latimer, but there was no certainty of it. He went on quickly, 'You're a great batsman, Frank, I'd give much ever to be half as good a player as you are. But I believe I'm a better captain.'

'On what evidence?'

'I'm more experienced.' He raised a hand. 'Think about it, Frank, I am. I've captained the 'Varsity. That's a difficult task, Frank. What's a 'Varsity side? Seven nineteen-year olds and, if you're lucky, a couple of Aussies or South Africans to give you some credibility. When we played the counties, success was to make them bat twice. It's like a grammar school eleven playing in the Football League. Run a happy side and avoid annihilation, those were the targets.'

'Not enough for a county side.'

'Keeping them happy's a recipe for a Test side, let alone a county side. As for the other, if you'll pitch in, we can do the annihilating.'

In the end he had secured an ineloquent acquiescence and from then on there had been no trouble. Frank Applegarth was certainly never free with advice, never sought to fill the traditional role of the senior pro, but his personal commitment could not be faulted.

Latimer came greatly to admire his concentrated efficiency at the wicket, the way in which he unobtrusively and remarkably quickly pushed the score along. Older members compared him to Bill Edrich, but that was perhaps prompted by similarity of build rather than style. His modest stature pre-ordained that he would be a good hooker, while the most violent of his strokes was the short-arm pull. If he lacked the willowy grace of a taller man, his cover drive was sufficiently aesthetically pleasing for all but the most exigent. But it was his beautifully-judged running between the wickets that Latimer admired above all else, and that, the captain thought ruefully, brought us right back to today.

If one wanted to make an instructional film on 'How to Run Between Wickets', Applegarth would have been an automatic casting. His calling was clear, quick, terse, he backed up well, though scrupulously within the laws, and he ran the first one briskly if there was the remotest possibility of a two. Years of experience had imprinted on his memory those opponents who threw left-handed, those whose arm had gone, those whose arm and speed were exceptional. Twice Latimer had engaged in century stands with him, and he was a joy to partner.

So what in God's name, Latimer thought as he finished dressing and looked down from the window of the Brunel to the rainy, empty promenade, could have possibly gone wrong out there? Palfreyman was a correct young cricketer, not noted for in and out running. The mistake had to be his, but why should honest error, even on such a crucial occasion, have provoked an outburst of such scandalous ferocity? And how was he going to lift the spirits of the side for the remaining matches?

He knotted his County tie and went downstairs to join the President for a drink before dinner. It was customary for the President and captain to dine together on the last night of the first match of Westercote week. This year it was more than customary, it would be very convenient.

In the bar he and the Brigadier evaded the direct assault of the *Mail* and the more urbane approach of the *Telegraph*.

'Nothing to tell you of any consequence, my dear fellow,' the President murmured to the latter. 'You can say, if you like,' he added as an afterthought, 'that we're greatly looking forward to the match with Warwickshire.' The reporter did not appear to find the last statement particularly engrossing.

'Shall we go in, Peter?' the older man enquired, and they

moved in from the bar to a table in a bay window overlooking the sea. Fairy lights strung from the lamps blinked and flickered dispiritedly on the sodden, anorak-clad holidaymakers.

'Nine-thirty in the morning, Sir Anthony?'

'Yes. That's it.'

'I wonder if it wouldn't be more private in the hotel?'

'It might, but it'd give you a hell of a gallop to the ground.'

'True enough. We may only get a preliminary investigation done anyway.'

'A lot'll depend on the weather, I should think. We might just have all day.' The President attacked his kipper mousse and changed the subject. 'You going back to schoolmastering this winter?'

'I think so. I rather like it and besides, neither New South Wales nor Victoria have made any offers!'

'Any of our chaps going abroad?'

'Young David's got a Whitbread in Sydney, with Fitzroy, I believe. And Frank was dickering with an offer from Border in South Africa.'

'If he doesn't end up in India with the Test side.'

'They could do worse.'

'After today?'

Latimer grinned. 'We don't know what happened today yet!'

'No more we do. Claret, d'you think? I remember, at Shrewsbury, what a bore Classics were, some fellow Mucius Scaevola . . .'

'Mucius of the left hand.'

'That's the chap. Talking of left-handers, when are we going to acquire a decent one? We're awfully predictable with our two off-spinners.'

President and captain settled to their dinner in a companionable bickering. Outside the rain drove the last holidaymakers back to even the least enticing boardinghouse, while in the bay wind and waves rose.

CHAPTER 3

The President

Sir Anthony Coverdale wasn't at all convinced that Frank Applegarth hadn't made his ground. He had been talking to Eric Constable at the precise moment, but the shout had alerted him and in the turning of his head he thought Applegarth to be well past the wicket. Damned close anyhow, and if there was any reasonable doubt, then that doubt should go in favour of the batsman. Not that he'd any complaint to make about the umpiring, always a difficult decision to give, the run-out, unless there was half a pitch in it. No, old Dodd was as good as there was on the list, and he himself agreed with what the master in charge of cricket at Shrewsbury had said, all those years ago. 'The umpire is never wrong, in fact the more wrong he is, the more right he is. There's no way else this game can be played.'

Shrewsbury cricket had been magical — it would have been even more so had one had the luck to be there when Cardus was assistant to the fabled William. He'd been fortunate enough to have a chat with Sir Neville in his last days about the old place, and it had been very gratifying for him to listen to the great man speak of the school with such obvious affection.

A kindly man by disposition, Sir Anthony had a briskness which made him formidable in committee. This was backed by a playing record which was highly respectable. He had played for the County from 1932 until the war, captaining them in the last two pre-war seasons, and with some success. By force of personality he held the side together through early summer after early summer until Jack Harrington and Martin Lazenby, schoolmasters both, joined the side in August, and proceeded to reel off 500 runs apiece in a month. Looking back now, the President realised that August must have been a grim month for such as Jack Horrocks and the other run-of-the-mill pros who had to drop out for the striped blazers and sports cars, but that was looking back, the 1970s surveying the 1930s. It had all seemed perfectly natural then. If the side was strengthened no one thought in terms of match fees lost or families to be supported.

'What d'you think, Eric? Seemed to me he was in. His bat was certainly grounded.'

The Treasurer inclined his head to the left in a diplomatic gesture of dissent. 'I don't know, we're not best placed to judge from here, square leg was in the way. I watched Frank as he came out. He was certainly flaming, but I don't think he was angry with the umpire. Young Palfreyman's for it, shouldn't wonder.'

'Silly young fool,' said the President without rancour. 'Still, we all do it, I well remember running out Jack Leeson against Yorkshire at Huddersfield when he was skipper. He was not' — Sir Anthony chortled at the recollection — 'best pleased.'

'Huddersfield?' said Constable doubtingly.

'Huddersfield. Yorkshire played there before the war. And a little bit after. You want to read your *Wisden* more carefully. If you did you'd know about A.C. Coverdale c. Wood b. Verity 114. My finest hour, Eric. A century against Bowes, Coxon, Macaulay and Hedley Verity.'

It had been his finest hour, although there had been other hundreds, a couple of appearances for Gentlemen v Players at headquarters, and a minor MCC tour to West Indies in the mid-1930s. The war, of course, had changed everything. He'd been living at home on the estate, thinking that of course he'd move out one day soon when big brother Geoffrey married. Like many young men of his class he'd joined the Yeomanry as far back as 1936, a decision which led to his being called from the field at Northampton late in the August of 1939.

He'd had a good war, in so far as there was such a thing, getting away from France in May 1940, spending the middle years in India, where the boredom was relieved by some excellent cricket on unbelievably good wickets, and coming back to Europe in time for the Arnhem offensive and the Rhine crossing. Along the way he had acquired an MC, DSO and *Croix de Guerre*, together with a pressing invitation to Colonel Coverdale to accept a permanent commission.

So he stayed in the army, played a little for the County in that first postwar season of 1946, rusty and out of condition, but so too were the great majority of colleagues and opponents. Tours of duty in Palestine and Malaya followed — in the latter theatre of operations he enhanced an already considerable reputation.

In 1951, when home on leave, he was persuaded to turn out in an emergency against Cambridge University. For much of the match it seemed a vainglorious error, for suddenly in the field it had become a long way down to the ball and his leg stump was knocked back in the first innings when he had made three by a persevering but essentially guileless Light Blue. In his second visit to the crease he was dropped off a gaper before he had scored, struggled and suffered the torments of the damned until, after twenty minutes or so, instinct reasserted itself and he began to time the ball. He made a flawed but battling half-century before departing to a good leg-side catch by the 'Varsity keeper. He was happy with his score and fixed in his resolve never to appear in first-class cricket again. It *had* been a mistake, and he was inordinately lucky to have come out of it with so little loss of public esteem.

He walked in through the pavilion gate, bat lifted in self-conscious acknowledgment of the unearned applause. He could see himself become a future question in these cricket quizzes that were springing up like weeds: 'Who is the highest-ranking serving officer to have made a half-century in first-class cricket since the war?'

He remembered pushing through the clapping members — people still came to the Cambridge match in numbers in those days — to be taken aside almost immediately by the then President, the Very Reverend Lance Fielding, and told that Geoffrey and Brenda, on their way over to the match, had been killed in a car crash. A tractor had come out of a field suddenly, causing their car to swerve and strike a telegraph pole. Brenda was five months pregnant with the child they had been trying for so desperately since their daughter Jenny had died at the age of three all those years ago.

And so, against all expectation, Kessington Court was his, if he wanted it, and he was astonished to find how much he did want it. It took a year to negotiate his release from the Army and thereafter he had enjoyed the life of a country gentleman, a genteel struggle but pleasurable. He had opened the house to the public on a scale and at times of his choosing, and with his army pension he made out, especially as the County had for seven years employed him as secretary.

Then, in the reverse order of the normal run of things, he'd become a North-Western representative on the County Committee, and eventually, by virtue of both playing and legislative service, he had arrived at the Presidency. All through his service career he'd been noted for his sanguine temperament but now, on the edge of his seventieth year, he had moments of gloomy introspection.

The house would have to go in a few years, it was too damned big even as things were, and there was no one to follow after. He reflected rather wryly that he probably belonged to that last generation of men who had the privilege of remaining bachelors without attracting the automatic label of homosexuals. He had given not infrequent proofs of normality in his Service days, but marriage was always something to be got around to, and never to be achieved. The house would have to go on the market, though his father had been entitled to think that he'd left things secure in siring Geoffrey and himself.

The cricket was changing too. Had to, of course; it was a harder world, a more workaday world. Why, when he came into county cricket, the amateurs such as himself hardly ever saw the pros after close of play. What a life it had been, going to see Noel Coward and Gertrude Lawrence after a day's play at the Oval or maybe the latest Cochran revue! At Canterbury during the Week there, they would go along at night to the Marlowe and see the Old Stagers perform. As often as not there would be a former opponent or two in the cast.

Brilliantine and striped blazers! Fellows like Maurice Turnbull, who led Glamorgan, and had once danced around that shire to raise money to keep the Welsh club in existence. He'd thought of Maurice today as he saw the visitors' flag with the daffodil emblem droop lazily on one of the pavilion flagpoles. Maurice was dead by 1944 in Normandy, Ken Farnes gone too: the three of them had danced to Carroll Gibbons at the Savoy after Gents v Players.

In some ways the game was better. His housemaster when he left Shrewsbury had said, 'Anthony, promise me that you will never be merely a *laudator temporis acti*.' He had promised at once, since he had not the remotest idea what was meant by it. He knew now, a mere praiser of bygone times. He sang a couple of lines from *The Mikado* tunelessly and softly:

'The idiot who praises in infuriating tone

All centuries but this, and every country but his own.'

Playing standards were higher than they'd ever been, no argument about it. Everybody could field today and field well. When he led the County there were three non-benders and at least one with no arm to speak of. If batting was less attractive, and he thought it was, that was because there were no fellows like Eric Hollies or Doug Wright about, bowling their leg-breaks like millionaires, looking to take wickets certainly, but always willing to give the batsman a chance to hit.

Playing standards, however, were the only ones that had risen. He could not abide the badgering of umpires that now seemed standard practice, but when he spoke out against it in committee, he sensed that others felt less keenly about it. He'd had to tell young Peter Latimer, too, that in his opinion only bowler and wicket-keeper should ever appeal for an lbw decision. He'd go further. Only one man, because he was straight on and stationary, could possibly know, and he was not a player at all. Yet what happened? All sorts of characters, from cover to square-leg, leapt in the air these days the minute ball made contact with pad.

Sir Anthony, erect, whippet-slim, stood under the cluster of oak trees in the aftermath of the run-out, watching the County go down to defeat. He exchanged desultory phrases with members, the ladies among them sighing that, if he were married, his wife would not suffer him to combine a blue/green Viyella checked shirt with the magenta and black stripes which were the County colours.

Life, he thought, seemed to come down now to a constant grubbing for money to keep going, to keep Kessington going, to keep the County going. Before the war the club had frequently been in bother, but it had never been anything that a half dozen or so fifty-guinea donations couldn't cure. There were times today, damn it, when he didn't know if he presided over a county cricket club or a vast commercial enterprise. He hoped that he himself was useful, but he knew that Eric Constable was indispensable.

The indispensable one waylaid him as the doctor's car turned out of the members' gate bearing the assaulted Palfreyman.

'I've just been to see Keith, President.'

'Indeed. And what did you want with our Hon Sec — or he with you, come to that?'

'I wanted to raise an item at next Wednesday's meeting at the County ground. I wanted to make sure that it was on the agenda.'

'Yes?'

'It's the whole question of the Festival, really. I don't

believe the County can afford to continue to play at Westercote.'

'You put that forward last year, Eric, at the AGM. It got
thrown out by a huge margin.'

'It may well suffer the same fate this year. But I'm working at it, drip, drip, Chinese water torture. It's got to come.
It's either that, or Carey Street.'

Sir Anthony sighed. 'Then we'd better discuss it next
Wednesday. You know that the mayor has invited you and
me to lunch in his tent tomorrow? Good.' Someone
plucked at his sleeve. 'What's that you say? Of course, I'll
come now.'

Constable, his business suit incongruous amidst the
tents and grass, asked 'What was all that about?'

'Applegarth and Palfreyman. Seems they've come to
blows, or at any rate Applegarth did.'

He moved quickly in the direction of the pavilion. On his
way he found time to remove his panama hat, bound with
magenta and black ribbons, to the Misses Ellacott, first
taken as schoolgirls to Westercote Week in 1924, and long
since life members.

CHAPTER 4

The Umpire

In the grey half-light of the August evening the Crippledyke ground at Westercote lay almost deserted. The groundsman and his persevering assistant were out on the square, pegging down the distinctly elementary covers. The groundsman, Tom Killock, cursed roundly as the persistent, slanting rain blurred his glasses and insinuated itself between the collar of his ancient raincoat and his neck. Why the hell the County had to leave a perfectly good wicket at the County ground to come up to play here, he'd never know. The canvas sight-screens were grey — black almost — while the outfield was used for hockey in the winter and it showed. The only thing that could be said in its favour was that, with its sandy subsoil, it was a quick drier, and from the way it was chucking it down at the moment, it was going to have to be, if they were to get anything in the way of play tomorrow.

Over by the pavilion, now locked and shuttered for the night, a light burned in a caravan standing in a little clearing among the gnarled trees which, whipped by years of

south-westers, leaned their spires across the field. Charles
Dodd spooned some instant coffee into two mugs, took a
kettle from the tiny stove, stirred coffee and boiling water
and handed one of the mugs to his fellow umpire, thereafter
sitting himself down on the bunk. The rain was loud on the
caravan roof.

'Day off tomorrow, Charles, I shouldn't wonder.'

Dodd made a face and added some sugar. 'Shouldn't
wonder. It's filthy black where this lot's coming from.'

His colleague yawned inelegantly. 'I can't say I'll be too
sorry. I quite fancy putting the feet up for a day, it's been
altogether too good a summer. Y'know, Charles, I haven't
lost a full day's play since Kent v Warwick in mid-May.'

'What about Sunday before last? That was a washout all
over, surely?'

'Oh, that! I don't count JPL.'

'JPL pays our wages, lad.'

'That's true, unfortunately. What was it Peter Latimer
said last Sunday? *"C'est magnifique, mais ce n'est pas le
cricket."* My view exactly. Four hours of bad strokes, nega-
tive bowling and bloody yobbos.'

They sipped their coffee in silence for a few minutes.
Then Dodd spoke, as if seeking confirmation.

'You reckon they've blown it then?'

'This lot? Yeeeeeah. Too many ifs and buts now. Brearley won't let it slip at this stage.'

'He's certainly a good captain.'

'Good? He's up there.' The speaker gestured vaguely at
the ceiling. 'There's Brearley and then all the rest. 'Course,
he's a bright bloke.'

'So's Latimer.'

'Sure. Not in the same league, though.'

'Not much in it as a player, Ken.'

'G'wan. Tell me that in ten years when Latimer's done something. John Michael's rattled up his grand almost every year for fifteen years. You watch him out there, he's thinking all the time.'

Dodd laughed. 'They didn't half give him a hard time at Bradford in the Yorkshire match last year. "Bloody MCC ponce" they were yelling at him.'

The other snorted. 'That only goes to show what ignorant buggers those Yorkies are. Well, they haven't been winning too much recently.'

'Haven't won anything. Can't understand it.'

'I can. Bunch of moaners. Knives out in the dressing-room. You can't pay too much attention to what's coming from the front if protecting your back's a full-time job.' His soft Hampshire burr warmed at the thought of old and feared adversaries now on a semi-permanent diet of crow.

His partner brought him back to present cases.

'Talking of knives out in the dressing-room, what did you make of today's little lot?'

'Well, we weren't there, were we? It's just what we've heard.'

'And seen. I saw young Palfreyman being led away. He should have an interesting face by tomorrow.'

'Old Frank certainly laid one on him. Have you ever known him act Asiatic before?'

Dodd shook his head. 'He'd a punch-up with Robin Lomax a couple of years back on a Channel Islands tour, but he's not a fighting man, very controlled, I'd have said.'

'There's something about him . . .'

'Oh, c'mon, Ken, there's worse than Frank Applegarth. A bit selfish, but a lot of very good bats tend to be that. It's a business with him.'

The other man nodded, half-frowning in irritation.

'There's nothing comes back from him, the word in passing, the joke between overs, nothing.'

'He doesn't dispute decisions. He doesn't slag umpires on the field or in the bar.'

'That's just it. Honest anger I can live with. I was standing with old Arthur in their match against Essex last season. Arthur gave him out to John Lever, a diabolical decision, would have missed leg stump by at least six inches. And Applegarth just tucked his bat under his arm and set off for the dressing-room.'

'Isn't that what they're supposed to do?'

'Sure. I just found it easier when I was dealing with the likes of Bill Alley. I remember turning down an appeal for caught behind off him. At Taunton it was, it was off the thigh-pad, but you know the Taunton wicket, you're looking for the inside curve. Anyway I just stood there, motionless, and Bill roars, "Jesus Christ!" I was a bit narked and snapped at him, "What did you say?" Whereupon he turns to the field and says, "Don't tell me he's bloody deaf as well!" A lovely man.'

Dodd went over to the stove and shook the kettle. 'More coffee?'

'I should be making a move to the hotel. What the hell, half a cup.'

'How did you see it, Ken?'

'The run-out, you mean? Well, he looked well out even from my end.'

Dodd nodded. 'It wasn't a difficult decision to make. They could have shown it on instant replay ten times and he'd still have been out each time. You'd agree there was a run there?'

'There was a run for Barbara Cartland there. Never entered my head there wasn't.' He smiled at the recollection. 'Never entered Mike Llewellyn's head there wasn't.'

'What puzzles me, Ken, is, even if young Palfreyman had been dozing, why didn't he call? It would have been a bad call, to pass up a single like that, but at least it would have saved tossing away a wicket, and you could say, the match.'

'I thought I heard him say something to Applegarth just as they came together.'

'What?'

'You wouldn't believe me if I told you.'

'I might.'

'I really am not sure of this. I'd moved from the stumps, of course, I'd a daft notion they might even try for two, that's how certain a single I thought it was, and besides, Glamorgan were a bit on their heels just then. So, like I say, I was on the move and he spoke quite quietly, it wasn't a call in that sense. But I thought he said "Goodbye."'

'You've got to be joking. "Say something, even if it's only goodbye!"'

'I told you, you'd laugh.'

Dodd passed his hand across his thinning red hair. 'What on earth would he say that for?'

'I don't know. And I don't *know* that I heard it, I only thought so. Whatever it was, it seems to have kittled up our old mate Francis.' He stood up, as did the taller, stiff-gaited host. 'Well, Charles, I'll head for the hotel, I think. Dinner will be off if I leave it much longer.' He cast another look into the dripping night. 'Horsey time tomorrow, I shouldn't wonder.'

'So long as it rains all day,' Dodd said lugubriously. 'It's the inspections I hate. Some of the members'd have you play in a sea of mud.'

'Yep, they never realise that there's always one captain

41

wants to play more than the other. G'night, Charles, thanks for the coffee.'

He squelched across the grass to his car, started the engine and illumined the dismal scene with his headlamps. The car swished to the main gate with its posters of Westercote Week, 14-20 August, v Glamorgan — JPL: v Glamorgan — County Championship: v Warwickshire — County Championship, and then moved more silently up the avenue to the town.

Left by himself in the caravan, Dodd washed the coffee mugs methodically then set about preparing his own supper, nothing more elaborate than a couple of boiled eggs. He winced slightly as his arthritic left knee played him up, and not for the first time he wondered for how many seasons more would he be capable of standing for the six hours a day which the first-class game required.

People laughed at him for staying in the caravan — one lady member this week had whinnied, 'What an original notion!' It wasn't an original notion at all. He'd lifted it, as he cheerfully informed her, from another of his umpiring colleagues, Paul Gibb. His mouth relaxed in affectionate, amused remembrance of Paul, who had eaten ice cream by the pailful, and taken an eternity to pronounce on leg befores — 'The Slow Death' the players had called him.

But he had cause to be grateful to him for the idea of the caravan; most of the counties were very good about finding a spot on the ground where he could park it. What he liked about it was that it gave him options. If he wanted to join players and officials for a drink in the hotel, he could, and he liked to do this very occasionally. He believed that it was necessary for a good umpire to be, not unfriendly, that wasn't the word, but detached, aloof. You'd make mistakes anyway but an unclouded, unswayed approach ought to ensure that you made fewer.

Ken was more gregarious and Ken was a damned good umpire, but then he'd played first-class cricket and was at the stage when many of his contemporaries were still playing. As for himself, he was glad enough after a day's fierce concentration — you had to remember that your error could cost a side a match, a player a Test place, a veteran one more season, a youngster an offer of a place — to stretch out on the bunk with a cricket book, or better still, an old *Wisden*.

He specially liked the obituaries, and had a particular fondness for such entries as:

> 'F. Pilkington Carew was in the
> Malvern XI of 1923, proceeded
> to Cambridge, where he played
> intermittently for the University
> over the next three years without
> gaining his Blue. In 1926 he made
> one appearance for Worcestershire
> and thereafter turned out occasionally
> for Free Foresters but without
> any great success.'

'Without any great success.' He supposed that it might very well have been the description of his own playing days. He'd gone up to Old Trafford in the very late 'forties in the hope of making a name as a pace bowler, and with wretched timing had arrived there in the same week as Brian Statham. Berkshire and the Minor Counties was as near as he ever got to the top.

Some of the players gave him a hard time because of this, not the top-notchers as a rule. Bernie Masterton was inclined to do his 'What did you do in the war, Daddy?' but

Applegarth had never made any reference, sneering or otherwise, to his lack of first-class experience.

He topped an egg thoughtfully. The accommodation was better now, but manners were worse. The pitfalls weren't the expected ones. He'd been warned when he started that to give a marginal lbw decision or a close run-out against a county captain was to court dismissal from the first-class list. He had done both at an early stage, and lived to tell the tale. He was glad he'd done it and delighted it hadn't been mortally damaging. It made him feel better about the game.

What would kill umpiring was trial by camera. You had to decide in a second, in a flying succession of boots, bats, pads, and from ground level, and when you misjudged, a camera positioned forty feet up showed you wrong . . . and wrong . . . and wrong. All the umpire could do these days was to pray that his off days didn't coincide with the tele-vised matches, and there was no chance of that in the Tests.

He'd have liked to have stood in a Test but there was little prospect of that now. Not flamboyant enough, maybe, not like old Ken who signalled fours like the con-ductor of an orchestra bringing in the strings. To miss out on Tests wasn't everything. He was pleased to be acknow-ledged as a good county umpire, and after all, not so many years ago it was extremely unlikely that he'd have been able to break on to the list from second-class cricket.

He sent a banana in pursuit of the boiled eggs and pulled out his diary from his jacket pocket. Folkestone after this with the other Ken, Palmer, for two Kent matches and then the Festival games at Scarborough. It would be good to get home to Formby by mid-September. Everyone thought you'd time and to spare in the winter, but there was always more than enough to do around the house after being away almost the length of the summer. There were classes to give for would-be umpires, refresher courses for himself. Then there was nothing to do but hope that your name would appear again on the list for the following summer. He thought that on balance it would, but nothing in this game was to be taken for granted.

He flicked the portable on for the close of play scores. Viv Richards had got 89 out of 157 all out, Somerset v Kent. David Steele was still kidding them out, 4 for 33 at Leyton. Only four notes of the pop group escaped his descending finger.

Quiet, and a book he'd been looking forward to reading for months. Not just yet, for someone was thumping the door of the caravan. A little apprehensive — you never knew these days with all those yobbos around — he called out, making no effort to unlock the door, 'Who's there then?'

'Tom Killock, Mr Dodd. Just to say I'm on my way. I'll look in with the dogs about midnight to see that all's well. We shan't need to disturb you. Goodnight.'

'Goodnight, Mr Killock.'

Mr Killock, Mr Dodd. His daughter Ivy would have convulsions at such formality. Well, he preferred it: it conferred dignity on the job that each did. He lit a cigarette and sent the smoke looping towards the ceiling, then sat down at the banquette table. He'd promised Ivy not to smoke in his bunk and he'd kept his word with rigorous fidelity. The book lay neglected for a long moment as he thought of his colleague's version of the events of the afternoon. Applegarth was not his favourite man, but if he wasn't a consummate artist, he was a masterly technician. It would be a thousand pities if he got himself in bad at this stage of his playing career.

Still, that was cricket present, and the County were welcome to sort it out. Cricket past lay before him in the shape of Jack Cheetham's *Caught by the Springboks,* the South African skipper's personal account of the marvellous series in 1952-53 when, on their own grounds, the Aussies had been held to a two-all division of the Tests. It would be a great thing if the South Africans could be brought back into the fold. He for one couldn't see why they shouldn't, though young Rupert Delaval thought very differently. Mind you, he was bound to, with his particular background.

Silent and rapt, Dodd turned the pages. Outside, prospects of play receded with every plangent raindrop on the window, but in the little brightly-lit space, Richie Benaud bowled to Roy McLean as the sun blazed from a cobalt Adelaide sky and umpires in short jackets adjudicated.

CHAPTER 5

The Striker's Wife

'Richard! Rodney! What's all that howling about?'

Alice Applegarth hastily dried her hands on a dish-towel and went to the back door. Two sturdy nine-year olds stood glaring at each other in the steady rain of the early evening. They were obviously twins. The slightly shorter one appealed to his mother as he stood clutching a sopping-wet tennis ball, his face turkey-red with indignation.

'Richard hit the ball over the wall into the long grass and wouldn't help me look for it. It took me ten minutes to find it, and now he won't go out. You know how Dad says it's out, Mum, if you hit it over the wall.'

'That's right. Give your brother the bat, Richard.'

'It was a no-ball.'

'Who said?'

'I did. His foot was miles past the anorak.'

'You're a liar!'

'You're another, Rodney!' The bat remained tightly clenched in the hands, he settled to the left-hander's stance. 'Come on, chuck us another one up!'

'That'll do,' said his mother firmly. 'I'm taking you both off the field. It's far too wet.'

'I'm quite happy to stay on,' Richard said doggedly. 'It's up to the batsman.'

'And *I* say the bowling side is being unfairly handi-capped by the wet ball. *And* I say the umpire's decision is final. Get along there now, both of you.'

The boys were chased to the house and ordered to towel down, in return for which they would be allowed an hour's television in their room. Alice finished off the dishes, came back to the long dining-cum-living-room, and sat down with gratitude. She lit a cigarette, glad that Frank was not around to disapprove, and turned on the big colour televis-ion set without taking any great trouble to watch it.

Her day had started at seven that morning when she had got up, given Frank his breakfast, and made up sandwiches for the boys to take to the cricket. The routine for Wester-cote Week was well-established. A neighbour ran the boys up for the start at eleven-thirty; Frank, of course, had got there nearly two hours before that, and on his way to the Crippledyke he dropped Alice off at The Grove.

He would much have preferred not to; he wasn't greatly taken with the idea of her working, and especially not in a café, even in one as good as The Grove. Alice was immune to argument or discussion. She liked the café — it was really a tearoom — and nine till two every day suited her just fine. She'd helped out Elsa Kimble in an emergency when the boys were four, and she'd worked every summer since, besides doing a couple of weeks at Christmas and Easter.

It'd been like a fair today, packed out from opening time almost, with all those people who wanted to see the County take the championship. Some of her regulars had found it difficult to get a table, though she'd managed to save a couple of seats for Mr and Mrs Johnson, a lovely couple. From Newcastle, she thought, anyway Mr Johnson often spoke of New*cassel*, but they'd lived down here for years. She'd fitted them in at her special table with Mr McKendrick the Scotsman. A charming man, but his lunch had to be ready at one-forty precisely, so that he didn't miss a ball of the afternoon session. He was a great admirer of Frank.

She wasn't. It was a good enough marriage, as marriages went, though dulled by rubbing against each other over twelve years. She knew his strengths, his shortcomings. A good provider, oh! certainly that. In a precarious profession her husband had never allowed her to go short. He was in earnest about his work, he kept himself fit. He was physically hardy — he would play while carrying injuries that would have sidelined other men.

Alice, while liking the game and well able to appreciate most of its subtleties, had never quite overcome her sense of amazement that her husband could actually be paid money for striking a ball with a bat. When the boys were smaller, he'd often taken leave of them on a summer morning with 'Cheerio! lads. Dad's got to go to the office!' He was self-centred — according to her brother Brian all the great batsmen were — and fretted over his infrequent bad patches.

Frowning as the mid-evening news passed her by, she decided that what she missed most in her husband was a sense of fun. He could try to be lighthearted, but his efforts somehow never rang true. His cry in the pub of 'Who's on the bell then?' had the counterfeit *bonhomie* of the man who knows he had a reputation for nearness amongst his acquaintances.

Alice stood up and, moving to the wide picture-windows, looked out at the last dismal light. Their home, a pleasant, unimaginative ranch house, sat naked and isolated beneath Locking Hill, a strange outcrop from the plain. The garden was interesting but uneven, the garden of a man who, although keen, tilled his patch spasmodically. Applegarth combined long absences with a disinclination to turn responsibility and money over to anyone else.

Sounds of a Western drifted downstairs and she smiled in recollection of the altercation in the garden. Richard, with his left-handed stance and exaggerated lift of his leading shoulder, was absolutely his father in a mirror. His twin, Rodney, who according to himself batted 'right way round', had none of the other's grim vigilance, which meant that the loss of one's wicket, even at beach cricket, was a physical pain.

People who looked at Alice Applegarth would, at first sight, if asked to describe her, have used words such as 'sturdy' and 'fresh'. It took a little while to realise that sturdiness was the impression conveyed, the actual figure was neat and disciplined and tall enough to have blasted girlish notions of the ballet. Her fair hair was short and neatly curled; wide-set eyes and a pleasant mouth gave her a charming frankness of aspect.

They had met in her local, The Swan with Two Necks, at Syaston, one night after a tennis match. Some of the County boys had come along to take part in a skittles match in aid of old Jimmy Richardson's benefit, and Frank had been amongst them. She hadn't bothered to change and was conscious of looking well in her short white tennis dress. There were no fireworks, no displays of gallantry or wit, just some amiable chatter and a request for a date. Then regular meetings and marriage at the end of the following season, Frank's first cap attracting the headline, 'England bat weds local beauty.'

Pretty enough, she thought, but no beauty. And since we've weighed Frank on the scales how about ourself? Passionless, their lovemaking had been far from unendurable, but not greatly missed when cricketing tours took Frank away for months at a time. Faithful, she'd never strayed or even been remotely seriously tempted. Just occasionally, when he was abroad and she watched a more than unusually erotic film, she would experience faintly disturbing stirrings, fiercely and immediately crushed.

For a long time now on his part there had been a lack of urgency for her. He had been very keen that she should winter in Australia with him when he played for two seasons with Queensland in the Sheffield Shield. Madness, of course, with the boys just about to start school, and she'd have to pay her own way. Yet he'd resented her not going, and she felt that since then he'd turned elsewhere. There were vague hints thrown out by others about his amorous adventures on the last Channel Isles tour. Not from Bernie Masterton, you could safely disregard that, all talk and no action, that one, so fat he probably hadn't seen it in years, but once Peter Latimer had said something, not knowing she was in earshot.

'He's deep, is our Frank. Never talks about women much, off on his own after matches quite a bit. I've noticed in this game the boasters are the barflies.'

He still visited her occasionally with his hard-muscled body, competent and unexulting when she wanted him, cool and not disappointed when she did not. The wives' section of the members' enclosure was a bitchy place. What was it Chrissie Masterton had said today? 'Young Palfreyman's girl seemed to be hitting it off very well with your Frank at the mayor's party the other night.' It was hardly likely that Frank, who had to strain every vertebra to out-

51

top her, would be of any great attraction to a twenty-year old who must be touching the six foot mark.

Christina was a jealous old bag, she'd be better employed getting a couple of stones off that husband of hers before he had a heart attack in the middle of the wicket. It was a wonder the cricket committee didn't have a word with him.

Alice hadn't reached the ground until just after the start of the County's second innings. She'd stayed to help Elsa get straightened out, although the latter had been clamorous that she should get up to the Crippledyke and see the boys take the championship. It had very much looked as if they would for a good hour and a half and she was hoping so, for Frank's sake. The championship, certainly, the nine centuries almost more so, with their testament to skill, endurance, willpower and, of course, luck. In his first century of the season Bob Taylor had put him down off a gaper when he'd made 17, and his Derbyshire team-mates said that he hadn't made a mistake behind the stumps from that day.

Many a cricketer she'd heard say that the luck balanced out and it had done so today. Frank was playing with complete control. His batting was never carefree, that implied a quality of airiness which he lacked, but all his strokes were functioning, particularly the short-arm pull which set the ball racing to the leg-side boundary. When he played that particular stroke she was always reminded of a sailor slinging a kitbag over his shoulder. He'd even gone for, and brought off, a late-cut, which he'd often scorned as a 'fancy-cap' stroke, not a 'business' stroke.

And then the run-out. She'd seen it, but couldn't remember detail. It had been relaxed watching, the County were scoring quickly, had time in hand, wickets in hand.

There must have been a run there, Frank would never have risked the dodgy single with the game in that state.

She had stayed for a while to see if the game could yet be won but then Peter went, and Bernie. She left at the fall of Richard Palfreyman's wicket, that way she'd beat the crowd out along the coast road, and make an early start with dinner. Frank would be very down.

She came away from the window uneasily, went into the custom-built kitchen and checked the oven. What would he do in a couple of years? Few, if any, cricketers went beyond forty. He'd never shown much interest in umpiring and, even if he had, there were exams to pass and an apprenticeship to serve in club cricket and the Minor Counties. She'd seen how old Charles Dodd crept subserviently around the pavilion, seeking — requiring — the good opinion of the cricket committee. That would never suit Frank, who had a contempt for the membership that at times bordered on hatred. Frank had talked of twenty thousand pounds from next year's testimonial, tax free; it was the equivalent of three good years' salary.

Well, they could use the money, the house had been expensive to build and was expensive to maintain. Applegarth had chosen the location, equidistant from Westercote and the County ground, adjacent to the Motorway which took him to away matches. In a couple of years that would cease to be a consideration, but the house would still look rawly set down in the landscape.

She walked upstairs where she was accustomed to run, and drove the protesting twins to bed. They could read, and in the absence of squabbling, she would send their father up to say goodnight. She left them playing a cricketing quiz game with cards.

He'd have been a sales manager by now, a head of

department if he'd been a teacher, an inspector maybe in the police, with twenty years or so assured employment ahead of him and, no doubt, further promotion. If he played five or six low innings on the trot for the County from now on it would not be attributed to loss of form, or even ill luck, but to advancing age. Only four hundred runs a season separated the majestic veteran from the spent shadow.

His car was in the drive. He came in carrying his cricket bag and a couple of golfing sweaters given by one of the County's sponsors. He set the bag down in the hall, slowly, deliberately.

'Bad luck, love.'

His head gave a short, angry jerk. 'If you can't beat bloody Glamorgan at home when the chips are down! Weakest side in the championship, although, fair dos, Malcolm handled them very well in the end.'

'Is that the championship gone?'

'Gone. We need maximum bonus points from our last two and I don't think we'll play tomorrow. It's pelting it down as I came out the road.'

'You might get the morning off then, Frank?'

'Report to the ground every day, no matter what, you know that. Supper ready?'

He ate unsparingly, happy in the knowledge of his freedom from weight problems. He looked up at Alice as she poured out his coffee.

'It'll be better if it does rain tomorrow morning.'

'How is that?'

'Fewer people around the ground. I'm on the mat.'

'What do you mean?'

'Disciplinary committee.'

She looked at him to see if he were joking, and satisfied

herself that he was not.

'Is it serious? You didn't say something offensive to the umpires?'

'I quite like umpires.'

'Frank, don't mess me about. What did you do?'

'I laid out Palfreyman in the dressing-room.'

'Young Richard?'

'Young Richard. And unless you're bloody blind you'll know why.'

'Because he ran you out?'

'Because he *deliberately* ran me out.'

'He wouldn't do that!'

'I've no doubt that's what he'll tell the committee tomorrow.'

'Who's on this committee?'

'President, skipper, chairman of cricket committee.'

Alice's face cleared. 'That's all right then, you'll get a fair hearing from Sir Anthony and Peter.'

'Peter pulled me off him.'

'It won't affect your position with the County?'

'No. I'll manage to convince them that my story's true. And they've seen both of us bat.'

He rose from the table. 'Don't worry, love. A fine, perhaps, maybe all the match money, that'll be the worst outcome. It's in nobody's interest to take this outside the club. I've been forbidden to talk to anybody about it. Are the boys still awake?'

He was playing the card game with them when the phone rang.

'I'm not in, and you've no idea when I will be.'

Alice informed the *Telegraph*, and then in fairly quick succession the *Sun, Mirror* and *Mail*, that Frank was out and she didn't know when he'd be back. He might even stay up in Westercote overnight. No, she herself had left early and yes, it was a shame about the nine centuries, but there was always next season, wasn't there?'

CHAPTER 6

The Terminal Case

Stephen McKendrick could still see the face of the surgeon, grave, his features set in unshakeable composure, as he sat behind the desk of his hospital office. Unusually for Glasgow, it was a still March day and the daffodils in a coarse blue bowl glinted in the tentative sun.

He'd read about it in a dozen books, seen it in a hundred films. Man of robust good health, starts to feel tired, loses weight a bit, has the occasional cramping stomach pain. Better see the doctor, go to the surgery, 'Hello, Mr X, we don't often see you here, what seems to be the bother?'

Describes symptoms, doctor examines, 'Well, it doesn't seem anything too desperate, but I'll just refer you to a chum of mine at the Victoria.' Chum wants him in for blood tests and other tests. 'We'll let your own doctor know.'

A week goes by, a fortnight, one begins to forget about it in the resumption of normal life, then a phone call to return to the Victoria to see the surgeon chum. 'We'd better do a little exploratory, Mr McKendrick, all sorts of minor things it could be, no use suffering unnecessary discomfort.'

Operation past, convalescence in train, still tired, still losing weight, increasing pain. Third appointment with surgeon chum, alone, at his insistence. Funny how the stock phrases could not be avoided.

'Is it more serious than you thought, Doctor?' Damn it, you didn't call surgeons 'doctor'. 'It is something I'm going to throw off, isn't it? I need to know, I'd have arrangements to make. I can handle it, Doct . . .'

And he couldn't handle it. When the surgeon had told him — since he made it a practice neither to volunteer such information to a patient, nor to withhold it if taxed directly — that he had a massive and inoperable cancer of the stomach, he had stumbled next door to the bathroom and been violently sick. The surgeon had been solicitous, patient, detached, talked naturally for a few moments of inconsequential things, all the while assessing his patient.

'I'm all right now. Sorry for that abject display.' Even as he said it he felt the irony of his apologising for having vomited at the news of his imminent death. How imminent was that?

'I cannot be precise, Mr McKendrick. You must expect an improvement in your condition, perhaps even a marked one for a while, what we call a spontaneous remission.' He shrugged defeatedly. 'That is the cruellest part of your malady. You must not allow yourself to think that this improvement will necessarily last. That is not the same thing as saying that you should not hope for it. But in so far as my experience tells me, you are beyond our skills. I would say you have very little time beyond the end of the year. You must decide for yourself when you tell your wife. I suggest *when* rather than *if,* though of course you will know her likely reaction much better than I.'

He had driven home, comparatively calmly, bruisingly

aware of colour, of smell, of sound. Yesterday he was a fifty-six-year old man, retirement an approaching prospect, but not imminent. Not like death. How did you cope with imminent death?

By thinking positively, the surgeon had said. You could die huddled up in mind and body, you could decide you would follow your normal pattern as long as nature would permit you to do so. Or you could do neither.

The following night he intimated his intention to retire from his post of Depute Head in a Glasgow secondary school. He would tell Liz of his decision and the reason for it in another month. Till then he would mention it only to the Head and enjoin on him that secrecy which he knew he could rely on absolutely. When his resignation became a matter of wider knowledge, he would simply say that, with the family up and away, he wanted to try to write something extended. He had already written a few dozen articles which had been well received; the notion was just sufficiently plausible to fend off the upsetting probing of well-wishers.

With luck, he'd be able to see the glens of Angus in late September, and before that, there was Westercote. He was half-frightened by the intensity of his desire to go to Westercote. It would be the twenty-sixth year for him, and it was possible that his exit would be on the highest of notes, a championship note. He did not begin to understand why that should still matter, but it did.

After the initial shock and grief, Liz had been wholly admirable. She cared for him but neither fussed nor smothered, she showed a bright face to the world, and she prayed for a miracle. Stephen wondered if she had perhaps a glimmering of the situation beforehand, if she had lacked his barrier of optimistic naiveté.

There was a long argument before he won his point on Westercote. For twenty years and more they had made their summer progress like Plantagenet monarchs. Spain or France, usually, a few days at Bournemouth, then Liz had caught the train north while he came on to Westercote. Not Westercote itself, of course, not a place to stay in, far removed from the beautiful cricket towns like Bath and Maidstone, more like Birmingham by the sea. His head-quarters for the Cricket Week was the Malt Shovel at Winterlea, eight miles and fifteen minutes out.

The Malt Shovel was a great and civilised creation. It had only four rooms, one of which was usually occupied by a member of the landlord's family, another would be taken by the new bank manager while he scouted houses, or per-haps by a visiting auditor. McKendrick was always careful to book well ahead, it had been his invariable practice to sit down and confirm his coming on New Year's Day, as if by the scribbling of a few lines he cast defiance in the teeth of the Scottish winter.

There was only one bar in the pub, three-sided, so that lounge and saloon were in the same large room but in clearly-defined areas. Depending on mood he passed the evening with building society manager and doctor, or with mechanic and farmhand. He always took a couple of books he'd wanted to read, and after the chat in the bar he went upstairs, got into bed, put the pillow to the foot of the bed and lay there, underneath the light. He'd meant to find the courage to suggest to George that the Malt Shovel should run to bedlights, but sixteen years of residence had not imbued him with the necessary resolution.

He'd told Liz not to be daft, or heroic. She didn't like cricket much, had never come in times past, and he knew he was obsessional about it, he wanted to see every ball bowled. And score while he did so. There were even more meticulous scorers than he, the six-coloured-pencils merchants, who could score and construct diagram stroke-charts while they did so. He wasn't quite as good as that, but he kept a neat and accurate score-book, and was accepted as the ultimate authority on the state of the game amongst that little knot of ten or so members that gathered every August just beside the sight screen at the Crippledyke end.

It was a strange relationship the group had — Alan the poet, Ian, the dapper little Inland Revenue man, his son, Jim, who'd a market garden, and the rest. They knew quite a lot about each other, yet they would have been hard put to it to write down each other's surnames. Every morning they faithfully kept seats for one another. They had set duties: one saw to score-cards, one got the hot gossip from the pavilion, one chipped in for the week with two extra tubular folding chairs. On the Friday afternoon of every Westercote Week they would retire to the beer tent at the end of the match for one drink, never more. Alan would propose the toast, 'Next year and a merry meeting.' then they would disperse.

It seemed now that there would not be a next year. He'd let Liz have her way in as far as she would come down to Bristol the night that the cricket finished, and they'd take three or four days to motor back north together.

He looked around the familiar ground with love. The tents of the various clubs, the banners above them, the Lilliputian pavilion, the flintstone villas that squared the ground, the light aircraft that buzzed overhead from the neighbouring flying field, these were the indelible components of his summer. The ritual of the game seduced him, the fifteen-minute bell before play, the five-minute bell, the

61

umpires shouldering their way through the skirmish lines of small boys, then the fielding side 'cascading down the pavilion steps like a white waterfall' in Cardus's lovely phrase.

They had been good days in the sun, perceptive cricket talk with his friends, whiling away stoppages in the beer tent with cricket quizzes and the selection of various great elevens. There had been a furious argument once when Alan the poet had declined to act as a selector of an Instantly Forgettable XI because, he said, to attempt to do so was a contradiction in terms. Funny how an Instantly Forgettable XI always seemed to be strong on Warwick and Glamorgan players.

Glamorgan had been memorable enough today, in all conscience. Even when the County had apparently been on the point of winning, he had been filled with a vague unease, it was all too glib, too pat, that what would in all probability be his very last Westercote Week should end in rocketing triumph.

He had not been attracted to the County because he was a success-worshipper, quite the reverse. The first time he'd ever seen them had been in the early 'fifties when they were no sort of side, chopping-blocks who could be knocked over in a couple of days. They had been thrashed by York-shire — an innings and 215 if he'd got it right — but he was enthralled by their very weakness, and his devotion to them had subsequently been unswerving.

His friends in Scotland found it difficult to comprehend this passion of his, that led to his pulling into lay-bys on the way home from school, in order to listen in tranquillity to the tea-time scores. Often as he did so, his mind went back to the large battery set in his grandfather's bedroom and a deep, pleasant voice. The retired blacksmith, twisted by arthritis, and the twelve-year old boy listened in concentrated silence while a man called Howard Marshall spoke of the doings of Hutton, Hammond and Hardstaff, of Fingleton, McCabe and Bradman.

In his jousts with the other members of his coterie, he made extravagant claims for Scottish cricket, and bestowed the title of Scot wherever he could. Mike Denness, of course, and Brian Hardie, Douglas Jardine couldn't be anything else with that name, and there was Ian Peebles. His friends were prepared to allow him Eric Russell of Middlesex and David Larter of Northants, although both had left Scotland when they were approximately five minutes old. They did, however, totally put the bar up on Rudi Webster of Warwickshire, on the dual grounds of being black and born in Barbados. They were quite unaffected by McKendrick's plea that he had first come to prominence playing for Scotland against MCC. Alan quoted His Grace of Wellington's dictum that a man's being born in a stable did not confer on him the status of horse.

Alan had defied fate at lunch-time by beginning to compose, after the manner of Dryden, an *Ode on the Winning of the Championship*. He had sat next to McKendrick roughing it out, while the Scot scored as imperturbably as his growing excitement would let him. His score-book was large and beautifully bound. The matches in it went back seven years, quite a little slice of the County's history, if you paused to consider. He thought that he would make some kind of an excuse to leave the score-book with Ian at the end of the week — just in case. It was always rather surprising to him that Ian, with his neat Inland Revenue mind, only scored on occasions.

Applegarth's dismissal had greatly surprised him. As the shot was played he had put an x in the bowling column.

He'd learned to put an x for a single instead of the figure 1 which could over-easily be confused with a too-large dot. He had been not only dumped at the loss of the wicket but angered, because of course the run did not count, and he had to make an untidy conversion of an x to a dot in the overs column.

His eye had been on the score-book really, he'd been tallying the bowler's analysis which, all right, he knew he should have done at the end of the over. He could not therefore pronounce out or in, but Jim, Ian and Alan were of one mind that Applegarth was well out. It had looked a secure run, but you never knew, there were always things out there not visible to those watching from the ring. Shame for Applegarth, shame for him too, he'd have liked to be able to say that he'd been at the match when a County player scored nine centuries in a season for the first time ever.

And, certainly, there was no-one more worthy of setting the record than old Frank. Stephen McKendrick's memory went back to the dark days of 1962, to a side with no bowlers and a tail that started at number four. Time and again he had seen Applegarth, studious, phlegmatic, not apparently put out by the almost total lack of batting support, graft out an innings of three to four hours which enabled his side to achieve a respectable total, if seldom a winning one.

When the last wicket fell, he remained seated in his folding-chair, completing his score-book, checking extras, double-checking the bowling figures, while his friends whizzed off quickly to tend their beans and broccoli. McKendrick could not fathom this hold which their gardens had on the English: Ian had been known to leave a game that was teetering in the balance to put in some work on his chrysanthemums.

He was packing up his bag when Mr Johnson, whom he'd last seen in the café, came towards him. They had coffee together most mornings, but sat in different parts of the ground, because Mrs Johnson liked the shaded area by the pavilion. Stephen looked up at the tall, stooped figure, brick-red at the throat and forearms.

'How to snatch defeat from the jaws of victory, eh, Mr Johnson?'

'I'm afraid so. The run-out did it, of course.'

'And the leg-before decision against Masterton. I reckon we didn't deserve to win at the end of the day.'

'It's a pity to see a whole season's good work undone by a piece of stupidity.'

'It was Palfreyman's fault, you'd say?'

'Has to be. A shot in front of the wicket is always striker's call. And there isn't a cannier judge of a run than F.T. Applegarth.' Johnson grimaced. 'However, from what I hear at the pavilion, he's perpetrated his own piece of stupidity.'

'How d'you mean?'

'They say he clocked Palfreyman.'

McKendrick frowned. 'I can understand how he'd feel, but there's no possible excuse for that.'

'I quite agree. We'd enough strife in the club ten years ago.' He prepared to move round to his car. 'We'll have to live a bit longer to see the pennant come home. You coming tomorrow?'

'Oh yes. I'll enjoy the game once I've gone back tonight, kicked a dog or two, got over my disappointment.'

'Don't like the look of the weather. Tide's on the turn in an hour and if it's raining then, you can forget tomorrow.'

McKendrick carefully put his score-book into a large plastic cover then bundled in his *Playfair Annual*, sweater and sandwich box. He smiled deprecatingly.

'I hope you're wrong. Four hundred miles is an awfully long way to come to see the rain fall.'

'Of course, I forgot. Well, mustn't keep Cecily waiting. We'll look out for you in the Grove tomorrow morning.'

The tyres of his car were hissing on the wet road as he turned into the courtyard of the Malt Shovel. He had to conduct a brief post-mortem on the day's events with George, who was a voluble, if seldom-attending, member. His infrequent appearances in no way inhibited his forth-right assessment of the County's playing staff.

'Could you take our Horace over if you're going across in the morning, Mr McKendrick?'

Horace was George's nephew, a graceless, gormless youth, whose spiritual home was with the Sunday yobbos, but who usually went over twice during Westercote Week.

'Fine,' said McKendrick over-heartily to conceal his preference for Radio Three to the inane banality of the chattering Horace.

'Much obliged. I'll see he's ready for half-past nine. He'll not forget being left last summer. You were quite right, I might say, you never get a front row seat at Westercote unless you're over by ten.' He produced a menu from a neighbouring table. 'How about the roast leg of lamb for dinner? And Olive's done a bramble and apple pie.'

Another meal, another pleasant night in the bar with Don Noble, the bank manager. Then, wrong way round in the bed, with the rain drumming loudly on the roof, Michener's *Iberia,* massive, marvellous, making the notion of Seville next year irresistible. All our lives, he thought, are geared to the blissful certainty of next year.

CHAPTER 7

The Selector

The thickset man in the houndstooth sports jacket and cavalry twill trousers had sat immobile in the members' enclosure for most of the day. He had a detestation of watching from anywhere else except behind the bowler's arm and the Westercote pavilion was, of course, side on. In any event people always chattered in pavilions and, as a selector, one had a duty to England candidates of undivided attention.

Don Rydings was as surprised to find himself an England selector as he had been to find himself England's wicket-keeper twenty years earlier. For most of his career at Northants he had been in competition for the England spot with Godfrey Evans, and that was no competition at all. Godfrey could keep in county matches as though his gauntlets were made of sheet metal, indeed he himself had played against him when he had been by far the better of the two keepers on the day, but always the Kent man got the selectors' nod. At times there had simply been no justifying it on current form, but not the least annoying thing about his rival was that once in a Test match, he would keep wicket like an angel, a player for the big occasion if ever there was one.

In 1959 after a couple of dodgy matches against India, the selectors had pensioned Godfrey off and looked elsewhere. They had not at first looked to him, and he was sure that he had been too long in the wings. A couple of young hopefuls failed to measure up, however, and he had lived to be capped thirteen times. It wasn't as many as he would have liked, but a lot more than he'd latterly thought that he would get. Don Rydings, Northants and England, had a pleasant air of solid achievement when the introductions were made at cricket dinners. He'd been on a couple of tours to India and South Africa, indeed no-one had been to South Africa since his tour. If they didn't get the apartheid business straightened out — and increasingly he thought they wouldn't — that alone would eventually guarantee him a place of sorts in *Wisden*, certainly a line in his obituary. He'd be quite happy to see *that* appear in the *Wisden* of, say, 2010.

That he might one day become a selector had never figured in his most fanciful moments. How the game had changed, he thought. In his playing days selectors were Oxbridge types, reinforced perhaps by a professional player of the highest quality, Herbert Sutcliffe maybe. True enough, Don Rydings was every bit as much an England player, but Sutcliffe was an all-time great, whereas he was someone filling in between the disappearance of one great Kent wicket-keeper, Evans, and the emergence of another, Knott.

After he gave up playing he'd got a job covering the East Midlands as rep for a gaming machine company. He could, within reason, make his own hours, and prospective customers were sometimes flattered to be taken to the cricket and introduced to celebrated names of then and now. His company clearly thought his cricket background advantageous, since they encouraged him to maintain his links with the game and continued to employ him. In his playing days he'd been regarded as a thoughtful player, a good assessor of the strengths and deficiencies of his fellow pros, with that eye for talent which is so rare an attribute. As a result of what he'd seen in club and minor games as he made his calls, he'd made several recommendations to Northants and at least two of them had turned out very well.

Despite this faculty, which he knew he possessed, the call from Lord's to join the panel of selectors had startled him, although he had enough confidence in his judgment to accept quickly. The offer meant that not only had headquarters respect for his weighing of a player's ability, they must also have marked him down during his playing days as a good tourist, a dependable chap.

So it was that he found himself in the members' enclosure at Westercote, sitting in judgment on his opponent and England colleague of time past, Frank Applegarth. He had arranged, through the secretary of the County, to pick up a pass. He liked to slip in unannounced to his vantage point, as he knew that if some players got word that there was a selector on the ground, their form was liable to suffer because they either went to pieces through nerves or tried over-hard to impress. Not, he thought, that Frank Applegarth was likely to succumb to the vapours, but he liked to keep a regular pattern, and there'd be time enough for a word with him at close of play if he wanted him. Meantime there was an objective and critical appraisement to be made of the veteran batsman as a possible member of the side to tour India in the coming winter.

In one sense, Applegarth was unlucky not to be in the

current Test squad, given the kind of year that he was having, but he had not been part of the selectors' thinking at the start of the season, and the young batsmen who were, had taken their chance against a weak New Zealand team. There would, of course, be one or two call-offs from the tour by the star turns. The Indian trip was above all the one that cricketers tended to make in establishing their Test career but, that done, there were always those who anxiously looked for reasons not to return. Hence the Chairman of Selectors' instructions to him over the phone last weekend.

'Better take a turn in at Westercote, Donald, if that's convenient to you. We could end up with a pretty raw side going out and Applegarth could give it bottom.'

'Is he available, d'you think?'

'We've no reason to think otherwise. Besides which, we don't know yet if we'll need him. Keeping our options open, Donald, that's all at the moment.'

Rydings thought as he watched Applegarth take control of the County's second innings, that being a selector was an odd occupation, or semi-occupation. In his musings he missed not a single nuance of what was happening out there in the middle. A selector acquired, or reinforced perhaps, an above-average knowledge of the cross-country roads of England. The match you had gone to see could be rained off, or the player withdraw through a late injury. A bowler might not get on to bowl, a batsman have a place in the batting order, which was not where you wanted to see him. Some counties were responsive to a wink and a nudge that the selectors were anxious to see how young X would shape as an opener, but not every captain was prepared to forfeit a possible championship to indulge a selectorial whim.

All down the afternoon Rydings enjoyed the spectacle of a truly professional batsman at work. There was little that was flamboyant about Applegarth, he merely knew what he was doing and did it unhurriedly. Play every ball on merit, run the first one quickly if there was half a chance of a two, take charge of the partnership if you are the better bat, in short all the eternal verities of being at the wicket.

Why should we take this fellow to India? Well, for a start, we wouldn't if everybody in the current squad signals availability. Let's assume there's a call-off or two. Applegarth is basically a selfish player in my book, I don't see him as a great encourager of young players. I do see him as a getter of runs. He has been in India before. He's tough and a thinker. Prepared, since the food might well be strange and upsetting, to live on eggs, chips and fruit for three months. He did that last time, quite cheerfully, or as near as he gets to cheerfulness.

Applegarth's phlegmatic, almost sullen temperament could be a great asset in India. He could cope with the home team's timeless approach to the game — it had always been his, Rydings', belief that in a five-day Test, an Indian side would bat quite happily for the entire five days, if allowed to do so. He played spin very well, and every Indian side he'd ever known relied almost exclusively on its spin attack. He would be prepared for the eccentricities of umpiring, by no means totally one-sided: he had himself seen both Vishwanath and Gavaskar given out to decidedly dubious lbw decisions at Madras four years ago.

Applegarth had, too, a curious if undemonstrative loyalty which would be engaged by any captain he could respect. Rydings reflected, as he watched the fielders change over, that there weren't too many of those around since J.M. Brearley decided that he had other fish to fry. No

71

matter, Applegarth could be relied upon to soldier on, grousing in the best British Tommy fashion, but not a man to go behind the skipper's back when things went badly.

Worth his place? Certainly. Here he was easing the County towards their first-ever championship, making runs when it mattered, against good bowling, against the clock, and on a pitch that was beginning to go a bit. That fellow Moseley could ping them in, too bad he wasn't English. No doubt it was the sun always on the back that gave the West Indians the joyful *élan* of the genuine paceman. That, and the absence of the trade union mentality, which told our youngsters that it was bad business to be a fast bowler in our seven day game.

And then, suddenly, Applegarth was out. Rydings felt not only surprise at his dismissal, but shock. He had begun to watch Palfreyman over the last few moments — one of the interesting things about selecting was that occasionally you went to watch A and ended up looking at B. Not that Palfreyman was even a possible as yet, too tucked-up, too prepared to let the bowlers dictate. Nevertheless, he thought he saw . . . something . . . there, and filed the name and the stance away.

Once Applegarth was out, he was able to watch the rest of the match in a more detached, more relaxed manner. He would have liked to see the County win, but their hopes had gone when Frank failed to make his ground. He looked at the rotund figure of Bernie Masterton with a depreciating stare. Good God! The man was a mountain of lard. He himself hadn't played first-class cricket for eight years and he was a damn sight trimmer. Bernie was cheating on the County, he opted out of sharp singles twice in the space of an over. Still, it was up to his committee to sort that one out, they paid him.

No one would ever fault Applegarth for lack of fitness, or for want of application. On tour there were always things to be done in the interests of good relations, schools to see and perhaps to coach a little, orphanages to be visited. Rydings thought back to the two tours they had shared. Some of the most extrovert, apparently genial players would go to any lengths to dodge these chores, but Frank had usually made himself available. There was no parade of enthusiasm, he was just there, talking naturally with the children, not allowing himself to be thrown by the appalling poverty which so upset some of the younger players in India. The Indians were very kind but extremely sensitive hosts, anxious to please, quick to take offence. Frank had rescued a potentially ugly situation in Assam last time out by rattling into two of his younger team-mates who were being abominably rude to a waiter.

There were, of course, difficulties about taking an out and out specialist batsman, particularly one who did not bowl at all, but he was good in the field still and, above all, consistent at the crease.

Rydings made his mind up. He would recommend Applegarth for the tour, and inform the Chairman of Selectors by telephone that evening. As he came to this decision there was a half-hearted appeal from Malcolm Nash, supported with even less fervour by Eifion Jones behind the wicket, the moving finger writ in air and Masterton waddled from the wicket, his face a thundercloud.

Straight enough, but far too high, the selector thought. You have my sympathy, Bernie boy, I wouldn't have liked that one at all.

He rose quietly and headed for the gate. This was not the time to seek a word with Applegarth; whatever else, it would not at this minute be a happy home dressing-room.

Glamorgan would win now, Malcolm Nash had his teeth in his victim, and Palfreyman as yet lacked the technique, or even the nous, to play a match-winning knock.

He looked at his watch as his car threaded the outskirts of town. Ten to five. He might just manage to make a call in the next town. His support of Applegarth, he thought, would be sufficiently powerful advocacy for the latter's selection. If he had a good tour, then he would at least start next summer in the England squad. That would make up a bit for the nine centuries missed, and the championship gone. It would also do him no harm at all if he were still an England player in his testimonial year.

Applegarth was never a man you'd reminisce about, in fact he'd no great affection for him, but by God, he was a time-served tradesman, brought up in the three-day game, where for every ball there was a proper response, and most of the proper responses were made with a straight bat.

Tomorrow, he'd look in at Hove, to run the eye over this new Leicestershire pace bowler. He was said to be distinctly nippy but suspect in stamina, prone to niggling injuries. Rydings sighed. Twenty odd years ago, as a selector, he'd have been choosing between Trueman, Statham, Tyson and Loader, but, on the point of feeling sorry for himself, the thought came that twenty odd years ago, no-one from his background would have been responsible for the choice.

He turned into a side street, parked the car in a lane alongside an amusement arcade and, in the act of taking an order book from his briefcase, pushed Applegarth and cricket from his mind for a time.

CHAPTER 8

The Reporter

Norman Stapler was not in good humour as he endeavoured to read his match notes in a poorly-lit public telephone cubicle in the St Ebba Hotel near the ground. At least, he thought, it was still a booth with a door, not one of those damned hair-dryer things into which you poked your head. It was, however, a booth which had not been built with his fifteen stone in mind. It was cramped, it was dark, it was hot. His troubles were compounded by three squabbling children immediately outside, and by a copytaker at the other end who appeared to be a candidate for Cretin of the Year.

'Stapler, Norman Stapler, S-t-a-p-l-e-r, I've only bloody worked at the Orb for thirty-one years. Okay, so you're new. I'm the cricket man, if you ever get to the back pages, that is. Here goes. County Championship, the County v Glamorgan at Westercote. I'll give run of play, then the score-card. Ready?' He changed to his dictation voice.

'One moment of late summer madness snatched the title from the trembling grasp of the County here at Westercote yesterday. Glamorgan walked from the field dazed, winners of a match the Taffs and we hardened journalists had given up for dead. Set to score 188 in 95 minutes plus 20 overs, the County, thanks to the steadfastness of old hand Frank Applegarth — that's cap A, double p-l-e-g-a-r-t-h — were within seventy runs of victory with seven wickets standing. Despite the panther-like bowling of the Black Flash, Barbadian — Barbadian, he's from Barbados — ends in os — Ezra — Ezra, cap E-z-r-a — Moseley — cap M then o-s-e-l-e-y — (4 for 47), it seemed that no amount of Welsh wizardry could prevent the home win that would so probably have ensured the championship. New paragraph. Then Applegarth called his partner, rookie Richard Palfreyman — cap P-a-l-f-r-e-y-m-a-n — for the safest of singles. It was then that tragedy struck.'

He broke off with a 'Hold it a moment' and threw open the door of the booth to address the noisy youngsters.

'For Christ's sake, move. Get out of here, go and make a row in your own room.'

The children, momentarily daunted, went. Stapler shut himself in again, dabbing at his brow.

'Sorry about that. Where were we? Oh yes. It was then that tragedy struck. Palfreyman refused the call and sent Applegarth back, the most hopeless of hopeless missions. The former England player was out by yards and with him went the hope of his side.'

He painstakingly completed his report, and went through the score-card, in which Llewellyn gave Charlie the Cretin great bother. At the end he said, 'Look, put me on to Douglas at the desk.' He waited impatiently.

'Norman?'

'Douglas. Look, there's maybe something happening down here. There are rumours of a punch-up between Applegarth and Palfreyman over a run-out. I tried for a quick word with Applegarth but he's apparently been told not to talk.'

'What's it all about?'

'Not sure. It could be just a heat of the moment affair, given the importance of the game and the stupidity of that young bugger, Palfreyman. It did Applegarth for the nine centuries in a season. I've put that in.'

'Have you put the punch-up in?'

'Give me a couple of hours to firm up on it. I've a notion of where I can find out.'

'Right. I'll expect you to get back in a couple of hours.'

'Well you might,' Stapler reflected as he shoehorned himself out of the box, clutching notes, spectacles and briefcase. It was a damned sight harder in the firing line than dreaming up headlines, such as 'Ezra's Black Magic Helps Welsh Wizards', which he knew from experience stood a fair chance of crowning his report on tomorrow's edition.

He lumbered through to the lounge and ordered a pot of tea and a round of roast beef sandwiches, contemplating his surroundings with a certain distaste. He was thankful that, despite the introduction of certain niggling economies recently — a re-thinking on 'overnights' for one thing — he was spending the week at the Brunel rather than this tatty place, full of steaming raincoats and clacking children. Stapler wondered morosely as he looked about him if there was any community of people this side of Szechuan that dressed with the drab uniformity of the British holidaymaker. In his expensive lightweight beige suit, tan shirt and dark brown tie, he was certainly somewhat out of place.

The sandwiches came, he ate them quickly and greedily. That had always been his trouble, he well knew; he would eat the four sandwiches set before him, had there been eight he would have eaten eight, hence his fifteen stones. Still, it was not entirely inappropriate, this solidity, this bulk, for a writer whose column carried, under the bye-line, the slogan 'The Man In The Know.' On this latest development he was not yet in the know, but he meant to be. He sipped and slurped his tea, breathing noisily, staring straight ahead of him while he reconstructed the events of the day.

From the purely professional point of view, he would have liked the County to win the match and with it the Championship. He was in no doubt that had they won this game, they'd have taken Warwickshire over the next three days. Then the story would have written itself:

> *End of a Century's Wait*
> At twenty to five this afternoon
> a roar of joy went up from this
> little seaside ground that must
> have startled shepherds on the
> high overlooking hills . . .

He wasn't particularly sorry for Applegarth. The man was a professional through and through, his technique was flawless, but he was not good copy. He could not turn a match with the sheer animal strength of Botham, still less bat with the feline cruelty of Richards. He never said anything memorable and what he considered to be quotable remarks were invariably secondhand. A mean bugger, too, not given to raxing the hand into the pocket where two or three were gathered together. Bernie Masterton had hit him off when he had described Applegarth — in the latter's hearing — as having an impediment in his reach, not, God knows, that Masterton's funny was particularly original either.

Norman Stapler didn't think, on balance, that Frank Applegarth should go to India, and certainly that was the feeling of the Sports Editor. The two men had arrived at the same conclusion by different processes. Stapler had tried to assess things objectively, and thought the selectors could do better; the Sports Editor faithfully mirrored his proprietor's penchant for the new and untried. In due time a thoughtful, unsigned piece would appear, pleading the cause of the young lions. If, as often happened, the young lions were figuratively shot during the tour, six months was a long time in sports reporting, certainly longer than readers' memories, and a second unsigned article would reflect on the folly of sending unblooded lads to the slaughter.

A sliver of tomato escaped Stapler's grasp and left a smear on his well-polished shoe, adding to his feeling of disenchantment and depression. It was a hard fate, genuinely to love cricket, yet to be condemned to write about it for the *Orb*. Outside sympathy would, understandably, be lacking. It was a well-paid peonage, compelling one to travel in a certain style to warm quarters of the world. He had not passed a winter in England these last twelve years. Yet he felt as he imagined Brahms must have felt, playing piano in his Hamburg brothel.

It was all right for the *Telegraph* fellows, and the *Guardian* and *The Times,* they were encouraged to be expansive, they had all the space in the world. No one could write properly if there was no space available. He found it galling that, because of the stridency of the rest of his paper, he himself was taken less than seriously as a writer by the cricket establishment, and was indeed treated with an unconcealed dislike. Not for the likes of him the coveted Radio Three appearances, but of course *Test Match Special* was the preserve of public schoolboys with an atrophied sense of humour, and professional cricketers of stainless plebeian origins who could be relied on for homely Northern fun and common sense. This cosy set-up allowed the public schoolboys to patronise the pros — some of whom became quite voluble about wine, on air — while giving the programme the seal of democratic approval.

Stapler rose, scattering crumbs from his lap. The toffee-nosed attitude of committees towards such people as himself was a constant source of anger. Without newspaper coverage, ample, free, they were nothing, these people, there was no game. Every summer's day the sport received a treatment in column inches, especially in the 'heavies', which it couldn't begin to justify from the numbers of people actually attending matches. It'd have made a damn sight more sense to print details of proceedings at the neighbouring bingo halls.

Meantime there was Douglas, and promises to keep. He'd have to think this one through. He had a genuine regard for professional cricketers, and a stubborn conviction that writers bore a heavy responsibility for their comments on them. What a hellish time Peter May had been given in Australia in 1958! He, Stapler, was in no doubt that the right to know of the Great British Public had forced a genuine talent out of cricket prematurely. Left to himself he would have told the GBP to get stuffed.

It was not, of course, left to himself. He went to the door of the hotel, looking out at the rain resentfully. It was hardly worth taking a taxi to the Brunel, but his shoes would spoil if he walked and briefcase and typewriter were burdensome. Reception phoned for a taxi, and in the few minutes before it arrived, he formed his plan of action.

His original informant on the fall-out between Applegarth and Palfreyman had been the score-card attendant who worked the pavilion area. A couple of questions had been enough to establish that he was dealing merely in hearsay; it was a useful beginning, no more. The two men involved were unlikely to be any more forthcoming. They would in all probability have been enjoined to silence by their officials and, even if it were otherwise, Applegarth had always shown himself to be a taciturn bugger. Palfreyman, too, exuded an air of self-preservation. There was a young man who, at a comparatively early age, had learned to look out for himself in the bad big world.

The taxi drew up just as he discarded President, Secretary and Treasurer as possible sources. The 'You'll forgive me for alluding to it, Sir Anthony, but it's important for our readers that I set the record straight' would make no impression. Sir Anthony and he were as one in their opinion of the GBP. Skipper? No. There were one or two captains of precarious tenure around on the county circuit whose first thought in similar circumstances would have been to establish their own lines of defence. Peter Latimer was not of their number. His integrity was manifest: in a funny way he was a bit of a throwback, a Corinthian, you might say. Any questions to him would attract the polite, amused stare which marvelled at the questioner's presumption.

So who's left? As he alighted at the Brunel, he thanked his stars for good fortune. His man, Bernie Masterton, was leaving, alone.

With no chance of demurring, swamped by the burly reporter's *bonhomie,* Masterton found himself in the deserted lounge bar of the Weymouth Packet, a mile and a warren of dreary side-streets distant from the hotel. After that it was technique versus naiveté, shrewdness opposed to gullibility, flattery taking on vanity.

'Bad luck out there today, Bernie.' He slipped easily into the garments of false woe.

Masterton contemplated his bought pint. 'Cheers! Norsman,' he said, and for the moment did not expand.

'I thought you were home and dry.'

'Didn't we all?' The wicket-keeper continued to stare into his beer. Above a dispirited gas fire, steam packets plunged and tossed vertiginously on various engravings.

'Frank going was the crucial thing, I suppose?'

'It didn't help. On the other hand, we're not exactly a one-man band. I'd have thought that blind bastard Dodd had a bit to do with it as well.'

Stapler blasphemed silently, enraged with himself. He had slighted, by inference, Masterton's capabilities as a cricketer. The next five minutes were now earmarked for the massaging of egos.

'I couldn't agree more. It was an outrageous decision.'

Masterton used a particularly offensive epithet, then said, 'He should be on the fucking Disabled Register.'

Stapler nodded. 'The press tent was in no doubt it'd have gone over the top.'

'Would it hell! Bloody Eifion had already taken two steps down the leg side.'

Stapler noted malevolently that the fat man opposite didn't only *talk* through his arse.

Aloud he said, 'Yeah, while you were there, there was still a chance. I thought you kept pretty well today, too. That was a good catch to get rid of Rodney Ontong.'

Masterton nodded, without affectation. 'It was a good one. Leg side and it only just carried.'

This was better, the touchy big fool was coming round.

'You must be in the running for the second keeping spot in India. I've hinted as much in my column tomorrow.'

There was a momentary gleam of ambition and longing in the other's eyes, doused almost at once.

'Not one of your more subtle nights, Norman. You

almost had me going there, until I remembered India and spin. I don't keep to sixty worthwhile overs of spin in a season with our pair. Milk can turn faster than either of them can turn a ball. The skipper's the only man who can get the ball to break sharply, when he remembers to hit the ground with it first, that is. And since when did the *Orb* influence the selectors?'

Stapler smiled good-humouredly.

'All right, then, Bernie, what's all this about a dust-up?'

'My lips are sealed. And apart from that, I wasn't there.'

'You must have been. You were out after Applegarth.'

'But before Palfreyman. I couldn't even bear to watch the fall of the last two wickets. I'm very sentimental about county championships. Comes of never having won one.'

'The score-card seller told me that Palfreyman had been taken to hospital in an ambulance.'

'Did he now? I wouldn't depend too heavily on what old Harry says. He likes to spread stories like that. It makes him feel as if he's of some importance.'

'Does Applegarth particularly dislike Palfreyman?'

'Does Applegarth particularly like anyone?'

'Stop sparring, Bernie,' the reporter snapped, irritated. 'I'm going to have to write this sooner or later. I'd much prefer it to be accurate.'

'So I tell you what happened, they find out, I get the bullet. Sounds like a really attractive deal.'

'I have never disclosed a source in my life.' Stapler's tone was patently that of a truthful man. 'It's maybe no big deal if it's just a simple punch-up in a pavilion after a bad call.'

Masterton raised his eyebrows. 'It was an excellent call. Frank called. Remember?'

'A mix-up then, if you prefer,' the journalist said testily. 'Is that enough to send a team-mate to hospital?'

'I can think of cases where it's almost happened.' Masterton was putting him down, heavily. 'We're sweaty pros, y'know, whether we play next season depends on what kind of average we have for committees to look at. By that time, hard luck stories are forgotten. They'll remember tomorrow if you're out to a blinder of a catch first ball today, but come October it's just another duck in the scorebook.'

'Come off it, Bernie.' He signalled for replacements. 'Frank's in no danger of not being re-engaged.'

'True. All he lost this afternoon was his wicket, a County Championship like as not, and an all-time County batting record. Why the hell should he be upset?'

'There's next year.'

'Come off it, as I seem to remember you saying a minute ago. He's only once in his whole career had a season remotely as good as this one. And the number of first-class matches is diminishing all the time. It's quite likely we'll be at sixteen four-day games season after next.'

'So what happened, Bernie? You were in the dressing-room together.'

The keeper flushed. 'He seemed to be under the impression that Palfreyman had run him out on purpose.'

Even his years in the game could not prevent the startled look on Stapler's face.

'You mean, deliberately?'

'That's what on purpose means, isn't it?'

The next twenty minutes were very busy ones. When they were ended the two men parted, Masterton to go on to a party at the house of one of the development pools' agents, Stapler to return to the Brunel. He sat in his room for quite a few minutes before he lifted the phone.

'Douglas?'

'You've taken your bloody time about things.'

'It may be worth it.'

'You'll let me judge that. What's kept me waiting?'

'I feel we'll want to think pretty hard as to how and when we use this one. This is what I've learned . . .'

In a rapid voice, pausing for the reassurance of consulting his notes, he told London all that he knew.

CHAPTER 9

The Statistician

Of all the people on the ground at Westercote that afternoon, none willed the County to victory or Applegarth to his ninth century more fervently than Simon Pollard. Like Stephen McKendrick, he had a score-book on his lap, but whereas McKendrick kept score, Pollard was a statistician. He was an authority — he thought he could say *the* authority — where anything to do with the County's playing record was concerned.

He was not prepossessing in appearance, being short and tubby. Two narrow fringes of black hair failed by a long way to meet in the middle of his skull, and behind thick glasses his squint was still disturbingly obvious. He was comfortably dressed in an open-necked shirt whose stripes were a pleasantly muted grey, black and blue, and his tan slacks were carefully pressed. Nature had denied him the physique to be a cricketer, and he had adapted by pouring all his energies and love for the game into the keeping of error-free records.

He had become something of a legend in the County and a feared scourge of the compilers of cricket handbooks.

There had been not infrequent occasions when *Wisden* itself had been forced to admit error — it would never have happened so often in Sidney Pardon's day, or Hubert Preston's for that matter.

He did all his talking and socialising at lunch and tea intervals. At all other times his attention to the game was absolute, and even calls of nature were to be rigorously resisted. People now knew better than to talk to him uninvited during play, for a turn of the head could mean the missing of an umpire's signal and an erroneous entry in the book, not the less annoying because he only worked at matches with a rough copy, and transcribed it painstakingly and lovingly each evening to the authorised version.

Alice Applegarth had exchanged a few words with him that afternoon between the innings. She knew him slightly because Applegarth occasionally consulted him on some past match in which he'd played.

'Good afternoon, Mr Pollard. Nice to see you again. I don't believe a match here would be accepted as first-class at Lords if you weren't keeping us right.'

'Thank you, Mrs Applegarth, you're very good. We're all hoping we'll see your husband score his ninth of the season this afternoon — and, of course, win the championship in the process.' He laughed nervously as the five-minute bell rang.

Alice smiled warmly. 'A lot of people are wishing him well, and the side. It'd be a first on both counts, wouldn't it?'

The small, casually smart man nodded forcefully. 'O.J.T. Manderley scored eight in 1924, but one of those was against a weak Oxford University side and another was got against the comic turns when Notts were bowling for a declaration. Every one of your husband's centuries

87

this season has been scored when it mattered.'

The umpires had appeared, and Alice asked 'Should you not be entering up our batsmen?'

'Oh no,' said Simon, pleased to be given the chance to expound. 'I never do that for a fourth innings where time might be involved. Too much chance of a change in the batting order, though I imagine they'll open with Briers and Cullis as usual. Indeed, I see they are.'

'You've really got it all worked out,' the girl said admiringly. 'Well, I'll leave you to it, Mr Pollard, I've got to go and find these two dreadful brats of ours. G'bye.'

And she had moved out of the enclosure, her receding figure followed wistfully by Pollard. Fit girl that, dashed attractive too. He suffered a moment's envy of Applegarth before, recalling himself to his task, he began to score with ill-suppressed agitation.

One actually saw records broken very seldom. His tally of major events was but two. As a young boy his uncle had taken him to Leeds in 1957 when Peter Loader had done the hat-trick for England against West Indies. That was something to have seen, no England bowler had done it since in almost a quarter of a century. Much later, the hand of pure chance, he'd landed in Swansea on a motoring holiday in Wales and on an impulse decided to go along to see Glamorgan play Notts, although he had absolutely no affiliation to either county. And of course he had seen Garfield Sobers thrash the possible 36 off an over from Malcolm Nash. Malcolm Nash, who at this very moment was clapping his hands and deploying his fielders to his own and Ezra Moseley's satisfaction. It could be a savage game this cricket. Nash had scored over 7000 runs in county cricket, he'd taken over 800 wickets, he'd taken nine wickets in an innings and made two centuries, and yet he was destined to be remembered as the bowler that Sir Garfield had carted to every part of the Principality.

The only other oddity he'd witnessed was Applegarth's best bowling performance, 2-15 against Hampshire at Portsmouth some ten years ago. True, Hampshire had only needed 29 to win and had a day and a half to get them, but it was a nice little statistical oddity when you considered that his career bowling figures were 83-6-399-7.

Simon's brother, Ralph, mocked his passion for statistical trivia unmercifully and quoted, he suspected that Ralph misquoted, a limerick at him:

'The son of a curate named Grover
Once bowled fourteen wides in an over.
It had never been done by a clergyman's son
On a Thursday, in August, at Dover.'

What kind of way was that to signal a bye for goodness sake? The fellow put his hand up limply as if he was scratching his ear. He smiled grimly as the umpire had to repeat his signal. He was willing to bet the score-box had seen it first time round and were just teaching him a lesson. He'd do well to watch Dodd at the other end, you didn't catch him standing on one leg like a wandered stork. There were clear guidelines for signals after all.

Sir Anthony passed by with an affable 'Afternoon, Mr Pollard,' but he had the inbred sensitivity to keep going. The dots and runs marched out across the bowling columns and batting spaces, the openers went, but at a good rate of exchange. There was ample time for the County to win the match and Applegarth to get his century.

Then suddenly, he was out. Pollard realised that his jaw was actually sagging in surprise. A batsman at the wicket lived from ball to ball, of course, but he had Applegarth's career at his fingertips and it was the mode of dismissal which he found astonishing. The figures were fresh in his mind, for he'd had occasion to check them only two evenings ago.

In 417 matches he had played 698 innings and had been not out on 86 occasions. Of his 612 dismissals only 33 had been run-outs, partly because he was such a good judge of a run, partly because he was merciless in ignoring what he took to be a bad call. Time and again Pollard had seen him calmly turn his back on a partner who had embarked on a rash venture. Surrendering his own wicket quixotically was not in Applegarth's nature. Most times, if you worked it out, he'd fallen in an arc between second slip and gully because just now and again he was inclined to drive a touch firm footed.

This had been the striker's own call and it was a perfectly good run, it was a most unsettling dismissal. What could young Palfreyman have been at? He'd already responded speedily to a couple of calls that while not risky — old Frank didn't go in for risky calls — were still considerably closer than the one he had ignored.

Sadly he entered up the time of the fall of Applegarth's wicket and the time when the incoming batsman took strike. There was still a chance, if young Palfreyman could get his head down or rather, keep his head down. He could earn himself his second fifty on a home ground if he was there till the close.

He was sorry for Applegarth whom he liked. The neat, compact batsman was a pleasure to watch at the crease. There had been prettier bats, Micky Dornan-Watkins certainly and Russell Stuttaford too, but Frank had been the rock around which they could froth. In a fourth innings, with only 100 odd to get, Applegarth would time and again come to the crease at 9 for 2, the openers gone, the doors ajar for an inrush of panic, and patiently, almost wearily, but above all safely, he'd make the personal 30 which guaranteed victory.

Nor, unlike many of his fellow-professionals, did he affect to despise figures as indicators of performance. There were cricketers who swore that they never looked at the averages all summer, yet in the time it took to run a sharp single to cover they would have worked out their own batting average to two decimal places. Applegarth used his figures as a basis for negotiation with the County. He made sure that he knew not only his total, but the context in which each innings had been played. A batsman who had seven 80s in his thousand runs for the season was almost certainly doing a better job for his county than the man who had two centuries in the same aggregate.

He'd not see Applegarth crack that record now, he thought. Too many ifs and buts. Warwickshire, who were in next game, had no sort of attack at all, Willis apart, but they were capable of running up 400 if they batted first, and few Westercote wickets lasted three days. At this time of year there was a fair danger at the coast of interruption from rain. There'd be some rain before this evening was out.

Rain was a nuisance at any time, of course, and he was lucky that he could go into the Ministry and, as it were, take back one or two days of his holiday entitlement if a prolonged wet spell came along. It wasn't quite the same, though, going on holiday later, it spoiled the shape of the year, and after Westercote, in the dying fall of the summer, there was almost no cricket to go to.

The increasingly rapid fall of wickets kept him occupied until the end of the match. He noted the fall of Masterton lbw Nash 11 dispassionately. It might be some consolation for the wicket-keeper that when he caught Rodney Ontong in the morning session, he had raised his tally of victims behind the stumps to 450 of whom, however, only 37 had been stumpings. Whether that told you more about the limitations of the County's spin attack or of the limitations of Masterton in keeping to the spinners was perhaps for someone else to say.

Glamorgan were not to be grudged their win. It was nice to see the youngest of the counties coming out of a long bad patch, if one could feel at all patronising to a county that had at least won the championship twice to our never.

He sat patiently in the queue of cars trying to negotiate the narrow gate, smiling tightly at acquaintances of past summers. In his opinion it was not the run-out nor Masterton's lbw that had primarily cost the match, but allowing Glamorgan to make 300 plus in their second innings. The fielding had been slack, the players on their heels, with Applegarth, Delaval and Latimer honourable exceptions. Even then Latimer, as captain, was culpable. It was up to him to ginger up the scrimshankers. Possibly too nice a fellow for his own good, perhaps the touch of controlled brutality was essential equipment for a cricket captain.

Ralph was coming round tonight. It was too much to hope that he'd be spared his gibes about ladling out honest taxpayers' money to undeserving Third World countries. The brothers were on good terms. He liked to think that he'd have chosen Ralph as a friend, had he not been chosen for him as a brother. Nevertheless, he did hope that he wasn't going to stay too late. His attention had been drawn that day to a paragraph in the *Guardian* stating that Middlesex's forthcoming match at Uxbridge was the first time that they would have played a home match at a venue other than Lord's since 1939. They had played their last pre-war home match at the Oval, since Lord's had already been requisitioned by the government.

Pollard's brow wrinkled in rebuke as he moved left on a filter. They had obviously completely forgotten the Middlesex-Hampshire game at Hornsey in 1959. He would write briefly tonight, pointing this out. You would think that, in a full-time job, they would have been able to get it right.

The chance of dispelling error cheered him. He drove into the bottleneck at the cattle-market thanking his stars that he was not a betting man. If he were, he'd have taken any odds against Frank Applegarth's depriving himself of an all-time County batting record by running himself out, or by allowing anyone else to do so.

CHAPTER 10

The Older Lady

At the precise moment when Frank Applegarth lost his wicket, Kay Manners had been rummaging in her carry-bag for the cardigan she thought she would need as the sun went in. She had therefore, to her considerable exasperation, seen nothing of the key incident in the match.

She would have to acknowledge this when her opinion was sought by other members, confirming their prejudices about stupid women who only came to county matches to exchange knitting patterns or recipes. It irked her, notwithstanding the fact that she knew she had no cause to be ashamed of her cricketing credentials. At school she had been a noted player and, but for the pressures of being a GP's wife and bringing up a family, she might well have made an impact in the limited world of women's cricket.

She often twitted Tim with the fact that she had been a member for far longer than he had, something which he explained away quite satisfactorily by his having been born in Norwich. 'It must be a big thing for you actually to live in a first class county,' she used teasingly to say to him.

She could have felt for the cardigan while keeping her

eyes on the game, but her bag was stuffed with all the para-phernalia — cardigan, anorak, sun hat, flask, sandwich box — which was necessary to keep at bay hunger, thirst and the English climate. Score-card, field-glasses and *Play-fair Handbook* were strewn about the grass at her feet.

It looked as if a good party was going to go wrong. Kay had begun to think ahead to the victory celebrations that there would be that night in the Brunel, or at worst, after the Warwickshire game on the Friday night. She was thinking how strangely things turned out, that she had booked in at the hotel for the week, and that she would never have done so had Tim been with her.

But Tim, string-thin, abstemious, non-smoking Tim, had died of an unsignalled coronary as murderous as any sustained by a grossly unfit patient. Two lonely years had brought acceptance, though resignation was something that would have to come later, if at all. There was no earthly point in commuting the thirty-five miles each day to Westercote from her home in the very south of the county then going back to an empty house, and the hotel was giving her a surprisingly good rate.

Last Westercote had been the very difficult one, it had required a definite effort of will to come. Countless people had come up and said, 'How's old Tim? That husband of yours behaving himself, Kay?' — and then been plunged into stammering apology. Trying to make them feel better had definitely been of help, and this year had been much less of a strain.

At her side, Bill Willock, an old Rotarian pal of Tim, snorted indignantly.

'Did you see that, Kay?' His ample-shirted figure wobbled with indignation.

'No. I was delving in my bag.'

'Hm. Bloody young fool, Palfreyman. Excuse my French.'

'What's he done?'

'Run out Applegarth by the length of a pitch. We'll be pushed to do it now. The fellow must be a mental defective.'

Kay semaphored with her eyes in the direction of her left shoulder. She pretended to go into her bag again and hissed at her companion, 'Two along, the dark-haired girl, that's young Palfreyman's girlfriend.'

'Oops. Wouldn't want to hurt her feelings. Which isn't to say he's not a clown and a dozy one at that.' He tried to make amends in the only way he knew. 'Would you like something from the beer tent, Kay?'

'Nothing in the way of strong drink. A cup of tea would be nice though. And one of those meat and potato pasty things if they still have them heated. If not, the tea will do fine.'

Willock touched his forehead with the easy familiarity of an old friend. 'Yes, m'lady, very good, m'lady,' he croaked in what he imagined to be the voice of deference. He got up heavily and made his way along the row, pausing for chairs to be pulled back and for sprawling legs to be retracted. Looking to her left, Kay's eyes met those of the young girl and she smiled reassuringly at her. She indicated the vacant seat on her left, and the girl moved along diffidently. By the time Bill returned from the beer tent, and that might be a little space, Kay thought, she would have put the kid at her ease.

'You're Jenny Monteith, I think, Richard Palfreyman's friend.'

'That's right. Have we met?' The voice was cultured, the tone puzzled rather than hostile.

Kay laughed. 'I was on the fringe of things at the Mayor's Reception the other night and heard you being introduced. I've an excellent memory for names, I imagine it comes from having worked as my husband's receptionist for seven years.'

'That must be a great assistance to him,' the girl said.

'Was. He died two years ago.'

'I'm sorry.' The conventional mutter of a sorrow she could not possibly feel. A pretty miss this, with the glossy straight black hair and the eyes that were almost cornflower blue. Rather overdressed for the cricket though, thought Kay, it's the boy that's the attraction. If he golfed she'd be pulling his caddy car round Westward Ho.

'I really don't know a great deal about the game, Mrs . . .'

'Manners, Kay Manners. Please call me Kay, I'll feel such an antique if you don't'

'My name's Jenny, Jenny Monteith. But, of course, you know that.' She flushed with vexation. 'It would appear that Richard has done something rather awful, or stupid. I heard what your friend said.'

'Oh, take no heed of him. He's a dear man, but he sees himself as some kind of peppery Indian colonel. He thinks your young man ran out Frank Applegarth.'

'He's not my young man. At least, not in that ownership sense. Certainly Frank had a face like fizz as he walked away. What did Richard do wrong?'

'I'm of no help. I was ferreting around in this cabin trunk at the moment of the crime. Tim, my husband, didn't half give me some stick over this bag. "Shouldn't be astonished if we found the twelfth man in there," he used to say to me.

'You don't come from these parts, Jenny?' The voice lifted at the end of the sentence, but it was a statement.

'I'm from London. Highgate. Oh dear, I shall feel terrible if we lose the championship and it's all down to Richard.'

'It's much too early to talk like that yet. He's still at the wicket with a chance to redeem himself. Besides, my Rupert's still to come, he can thrash them a bit on his day.'

'Rupert Delaval? The . . . West Indian boy?'

Kay nodded, as she welcomed the returning Bill, pint in one hand, plastic cup in the other, transferring a proportion of the contents of both to the trampled grass.

'Jenny, this is Mr Bill Willock. Bill, this is Jenny Monteith.' Both those being introduced expressed pleasure.

It was shortly after this that Richard Palfreyman fell. Kay sighed. 'Rupert's the hope of the side now. Here he comes.' She raised her voice in exhortation. 'Come on, Rupert, give them stick.'

Those around her smiled at the big-made, fiftyish lady in the sundress, and the batsman, picking up the voice, smiled warmly in her direction.

The approach from the County Committee to see if she would take in Rupert Delaval for a few settling-in months had come unexpectedly to Kay, who was then in her second year as a South Area Committee member. It was an outward sign of acceptance, that her past as a Supporters' Association stalwart — at a time when relations between County and Association were very frigid — was no longer to be held against her.

Tim had been all for the idea, and God knows there was room enough now that Ivor was married up in Middlesbrough and Gareth had gone off to Exeter University. The whippy black figure, whom they had met off the London train on an avengingly cold April day, had made their house his home for the whole of his first qualifying season. He was a quiet, affectionate lad with beautiful manners.

Tim and he had hit it off from the start — conversation was never stilted or uneasy. He was desperately anxious not to give extra work: it was several weeks before she discovered that when he went out in the evenings he had nowhere to go and that he tramped the redbrick terrace streets for hours in the numbing spring winds rather than be 'under their feet'.

Rupert had needed, if not fattening, at least filling out, and he had needed encouragement in those first few months, when the decision to try his luck on the county circuit seemed at times to him to have been a horrendous mistake. Even when he moved out to a flat of his own, he still came round regularly. In her handbag was the letter he'd written from Antigua when he learned of Tim's death, the untutored phrases more moving than any formal panegyric.

And, at the end of the current season, there was his wedding to look forward to, the invitation having arrived just the other day. She knew the girl, Tilly Dempster, well, and from her heart out wished them happiness, though not without unease. People were more sensible than they used to be about such things, but a black-white marriage would always provide a field day for the malicious.

She supposed she did look on him as a kind of adopted son, rather. The odd bits of maintenance and repair around the house, which were a worrying consideration now that Tim was gone, were dealt with by Rupert expeditiously and neat-handedly. When the County were in the field he used to look for her, and if he was in the deep, position himself as close as captain and bowler would allow. Kay never grew tired of seeing him stoop to the ball, gather and then hurl it like a skimming swallow to the 'keeper.

Since he came to England there had only once been a brief coldness between them. He had come back to the

99

house twice in quick succession having clearly drunk rather too much. Bernie Masterton and Frank Applegarth, she'd be bound, not a pair of whom she was inordinately fond. Masterton was a dangerous influence because he could sup gargantuan quantities of beer without changing expression, as many a cricketing innocent had discovered to his financial and physical cost. Applegarth she lost the taste for after hearing him in the lunch tent one day rattle off a stream of very blue jokes while not so much unaware of as actively enjoying the embarrassment of the young schoolgirl who was waiting at table.

Rupert came to the wicket, hit out and perished nobly as the innings subsided in defeat. Jenny Monteith, with a sigh, stood up to go, making a long face.

'I'm not looking forward to this evening. There'll be no living with Richard.'

I imagine there has been some living with Richard, Kay thought, and immediately chided herself. It didn't follow, even today's youngsters were often more forward in speech than deed, and in any event, it was no concern of hers.

Aloud she said, 'I should get him to take you out to dinner, somewhere away from the Brunel. If he stays there it will be post-mortems and crying into the beer all night.'

The girl nodded doubtfully. 'He's bound to be depressed, and with reason. Richard's not by any means established in the side, and now he lets them down like this. Of all people it had to be Frank Applegarth.'

'Don't they get on?'

'Not particularly. Richard says that Frank treats him as a drill sergeant would treat a not very bright recruit.'

Kay smiled benevolently. 'He's a very nice young man, he shouldn't let that sourpuss affect him. Even if he did goof this afternoon, it's nothing that hasn't happened to much more famous players. It was very nice to talk to you, Jenny.' She turned to her other side where Bill Willock was catching up on yesterday's cricket in the *Guardian*. 'Jenny's going, Bill.'

Bill lumbered up from the depths of his deck chair and took his leave awkwardly.

'Nice looking girl, that,' he said. 'Can't think what she sees in Palfreyman.'

'I can.'

'Hm. Well. I was thinking, Kay, I might stay up at Westercote this evening for a bit. Perhaps we could break bread together at the Brunel?'

'Thanks, Bill, but I don't think so tonight. Got a bit of a head, actually. I know exactly how I came by it, squinting into the sun without bothering to put my sunglasses on. So that's a headache *and* crow's feet. At least an early night will cure the headache.'

'There's not a crow's foot in sight,' said Bill gallantly and untruthfully. 'Pity about tonight. You coming down tomorrow, Kay?'

'Of course. That's when we'll need our real supporters. The fairweather friends will take wing after today. I'll see you around noon. I've got one or two things to do up town first. Drive safely.'

She set off briskly for the hotel. It would not be long before Bill asked her out formally, and she would have to think how her refusal could be as little hurtful as possible. A fifty-five year old bachelor was a big hostage to fortune, in Bill's case and given his girth, a gigantic hostage to fortune.

Tim had occasionally talked with her about what they would do if one or the other died, as if there were any 'if' about it. Each had agreed not to discount the possibility of remarrying, 'not much of an advert for us if we thought

101

otherwise,' Tim used to joke. So, she would wait, and she would see. There were little areas of freedom that she had grown to value, though much of the fun had gone with Tim. Bill had a good heart beneath that blustering facade, but if she ever married again, it would be someone as yet undiscerned. She made a mental note to phone Ivor and Dorothy at Middlesbrough later in the evening. They were staying overnight with her next week en route to Devon for the holidays, which meant at least a few hours with her young rip of a grandson, Graham. She went through the swing doors of the Brunel smiling ruefully at the thought of Bill Willock courting a grannie.

CHAPTER 11

The Scorers

In their hideously uncomfortable little wooden box Idris Morgan and Matthew Hardie discharged their function as official scorers, looking for all the world like Dickensian clerks as they sat on wooden chairs at their broad, sloping ledges. From time to time they exchanged brief, business-like comments, confirming a signal or checking a bowling analysis.

'Four off the last over, Matthew?'

'That's right. Dot, dot, 1, dot, 3, dot.'

'Moseley now reads 14-5-31-3?'

'Check.'

Both men, if asked, would have found it odd that the Laws of Cricket deigned to take so little notice of their work, Law 4 dismissing their rôle as merely being that of recording the runs and acknowledging the signals. They would have said that their rôle was every bit as important as that of the umpires, and their impartiality quite as rigorous. There was not a scorer in the first class game who would not, in the interests of truth, find against his own county.

It was a job for quiet men, men who were phlegmatic, methodical, easy-going. The latter quality was essential if you were going to spend three working days on end cooped up in a birdcage whose dimensions would have made a prison cell seem spacious.

'Worse in the old days, Matthew, see?' said Idris reflectively at the fall of a wicket. 'When we used to take the matches all round the county, to Neath, to bloody Ponty, to Ebbw Vale. We scored in tents, sitting in the open on platforms, all sorts, boy. Some of the English grounds weren't any better, mind you.'

Matthew Hardie smiled. 'I'm not sorry to have missed out on those, Idris, though I think it's a pity we don't take the game out more. County ground and here, that's about it these days. Some of the smaller grounds must have been fun though?'

'Don't you believe it, boy. I've seen old score-books streaked with grime when the wind blew ash and coal dust from the bings. There was a Northants player just before the war, R.P. Nelson, the skipper, good player, he was killed, and he's supposed to have said that he'd come next time in a dinner-suit to save his whites.'

Hardie consulted his watch and the pavilion clock. 'Rupert Delaval in at 5.19 p.m.?'

'5.19 it is.'

'I thought we'd have seen history made here today.'

'Not now.' As the bowler started his run up, the Welshman nudged admonishingly, 'Back to work.'

Three day cricket required, of course, unremitting attention on the part of the scorers, but it was an altogether more scholarly process than the one-day matches. Nat West and Benson and Hedges weren't quite so bad, the former was a perfectly decent day's cricket and the crowds, though large and noisy, were basically cricket crowds and fairly well behaved. As for the B & H, the qualifying matches were played early in the season in midweek, before a comparative handful of spectators.

Sundays, though, were hell on wheels. Because of the limitation on bowlers' run-ups, sides got through the overs much faster, the incidence of extras was high, and the behaviour of the crowd was frequently appalling. It wasn't the first time that they had had to station a policeman immediately outside the score-box to prevent young boys or older clowns keeping up an incessant drumming on the planks throughout the afternoon. Hardie agreed with his vis-à-vis that it was totally baffling why these people came to the ground at all. They appeared to have no great love for cricket, and it was painfully obvious that they had very little understanding of it.

Any scorer worth his salt would much prefer the tranquillity of the Wednesday morning on which midweek county games started. That gave him time to do other things, such as lift the phone to the score-board and keep the operators in order. Westercote, in this, presented unusual difficulties. The smaller score-board, next to the scorers, but outwith their line of vision, was fine, quick to respond to umpire's signal or scorers' ring. The larger board, leering at them from across the ground, was a disaster. It was reliable before the first ball of the Festival was bowled, when it read 0 for 0, Batsman 1,0, Batsman 2,0. Thereafter, if its totals coincided with the actual state of play, it was as likely as not a happy accident. The Welsh scorer had a theory for it which he had propounded to Hardie the previous day.

'I reckon they wait till the O Levels are out, right? Then they look for the six boys who have done worst in Arithmetic. When they have 'em, they pick the two who know least about cricket, especially about umpire's signals. It's the only theory that fits the case.'

It was said goodhumouredly enough, but Matthew Hardie was nettled because he recognised the basic truth of the criticism. He had beavered away at Eric Constable for some time now, urging that he obtain the services of some club score-board man — God knows there were enough people of retirement age to fit the bill. They could pay him something nominal like a fiver a day and meals. Giving whoever it was a complimentary membership would be even better. Constable, the careful steward, preferred to stick with his two schoolboys, who could be bought with lemonade and sandwiches — and who could be relied on to make a mess of things.

The two men had come to scoring at different times and by different routes. Hardie had been in the job for three years, his background village cricket, his availability the result of his recent retirement from his fishmonger's business. He was still a little in awe of some of the more famous and experienced scorers, amongst whom he willingly included Idris Morgan. Idris had almost made it, being in the Glamorgan Second XI in their great championship year of 1948, when the entries on the score-sheet had grown marginally shakier as the daffodil caps edged towards the title. Realising that as a player he was just going to fall short, and wishing to stay in the game, he had jumped at the chance of becoming county scorer in the early 'fifties. In the winter he helped with the Development Fund and the organisation of Sportsmen's Evenings, and every summer he went on his Grand Tour. Watkins, Pressdee, Majid, Tony Lewis, Javed, he had recorded their frequent triumphs and much rarer failures.

Don Rydings had paid them a visit over the lunch interval. He often, when running the rule over a player, had a word with the scorer who, above all people, was certain to have seen the bowler bowl every ball, the batsman face each delivery. He had been impressed by what he had learned from Matthew Hardie about Applegarth.

'He's not only got runs, he's never looked like getting out. It's almost soothing to watch him. He just stays there and the board ticks over.'

'Who's given him trouble, in your opinion?'

'Joel Garner most of all. It was a dicey Bath wicket though, and big Joel does bring them down from nine feet or so.'

'How many did he get?'

'Thirty-one in two hours all but five minutes. He was playing most of them off breastbone and throat.'

The selector nodded abstractedly. 'Anyone else, Mr Hardie?'

'Sylvester Clarke, till he got his bearings. Certainly no spinners to speak of. Oddly enough, David Steele kept him quieter than most.'

'That's not so odd. He's a very underrated bowler is David. Always has been. Anyway, thanks for that, you've been very helpful. We'll see if he gets his record.' With a wave of the hand he went back to the members' enclosure.

The fall of Applegarth's wicket brought a long whistle from Idris Morgan. 'Who would I not like to be at this moment, boy? Young Mr Palfreyman, that's who. I remember a chap coming to play for Glamorgan, joined us from Worcestershire. In his very first match, he runs out the skipper, Wilf Wooller. You remember old Wilf?'

'Vividly,' Matthew Hardie murmured.

'Well, this fellow, he's so scared of Wilf, and it's just

107

before lunch, he daren't go in the lunch tent. Someone brings him out a sandwich eventually.' His voice became thoughtful in tone. 'I don't think he lasted very long with us.'

Hardie had a dim idea of how enraged and disappointed Frank Applegarth would be at this moment. His hunger for runs was unappeasable, it was precisely this fact which made him such a formidable opponent. In the Kent match a couple of weeks ago, the umpire had signalled four leg byes from a ball of great speed in the third over from Graham Dilley. At the tea interval, Applegarth had let it be known to the scorers that he had got a faint inside edge on it and that once again the myopia of umpires had served him ill. The Kent scorer — Matthew wished for his courage — had rejoined, 'Too bad, Frank. No doubt you'd have been walking if Knotty had caught it,' — a shrewd thrust since the complainant was not renowned for making the umpire's job easier, although he rarely dissented.

Mistakes happened. Idris had claimed, over a pint the previous evening, that he had scored in a game where there had been a hat trick of run-outs, if you could have a hat trick of run-outs, and that for good measure, one of them had been off a no ball. He gave chapter and verse, but Matthew determined to look it up just the same; he had no recollection of ever reading about such an event.

The match ended, and somewhat selfconsciously, the two scorers shook hands, rather as drummer-boys in eighteenth-century armies might in contrast have joined in the fray. Charles Dodd came over to check and finalise the score, part of the duties enjoined upon umpires. The book-keeping was perfect in every aspect. Certainly there was always more possibility of a discrepancy in really tight finishes, but Hardie disliked intensely the very occasional situation where both scorers were grubbing around in their books, looking for an extra to reconcile the tally.

That had happened, he seemed to remember, when Holmes and Sutcliffe made 555 for the first wicket for Yorkshire at Leyton in 1932, thus beating the previous record of 554 by Brown and Tunnicliffe. Only, there was some doubt if they had done so, one of the books stubbornly read 554, and Yorkshire had already declared on the strength of the record. Eventually they found an extra — had it been a bye? — and they agreed on the larger total, but he had never been totally convinced by it.

No doubt it had happened quite a lot in the Hambledon days, as the scorers sat on benches, high up in the Downs, whittling the notches to an accompaniment of larksong. They had begun the craft which had developed to the point where Bill Frindall was a cricketing personality in his own right, pouring out in a molten lava stream bowling details, run rates, number of balls faced, whilst all the time sustaining a Johnsonian barrage of relentless fatuity.

It was time for leave-taking, in this strange little world of professional cricket, involving at most some five hundred people. They, the scorers, would meet once next season anyhow, in Wales, the fixtures decreed. Depending on cup draws, their paths might cross again.

'Nice to see you again, Matthew. Sorry you couldn't just do it at the end of the day. I think we'd rather you'd won it than Middlesex.'

'I don't know. Their captain's pretty well out on his own, isn't he?'

'Oh, indeed, yes. But they're from the big city and we're simple country lads, you know.' He brightened visibly. 'Still, as long as bloody Yorkshire don't win it any of the other fifteen are welcome to it.' He stood up, sticking pens in his pocket, cramming a disreputable soft hat on his head, ready for the road. 'See you at Swansea next season.'

'Three day match and JPL.'

'Check. I hear they're thinking of taking the Sunday match to one of the smaller grounds.'

'Use all your influence to stop them, Idris.'

'Go on, man. If you haven't scored at Ponty you haven't bloody well lived.'

'I'll try to bear the loss,' the County scorer said stolidly. 'Good game of cricket though, wasn't it?'

CHAPTER 12

The Hotel Manager

Dermot Riordan, coming towards the end of his third year as manager of the Brunel Hotel, was actively seeking a shift. It was not that he disliked the place. On the contrary, he had come to be fond of the great, gaunt, grey-turreted pile which dwarfed all the roadhouse architecture of the sea-front, a dowager dropped among suburban housewives at a coffee morning.

No, it was simply that there were tours of duty in hotel management as in all else, and he had made his best contribution to the Brunel by this time.

'Evening, Sir Anthony, Mr Latimer.'

'Good evening to you.'

Riordan, tall, his high colouring sitting oddly on a face that was lean to the point of asceticism, congratulated himself quietly on getting their names right as the two men disappeared towards the dining-room. It was an important card in an hotelier's hand, the ability to put a name to guests, but it was not, for him, a gift. He had, over the years, worked hard at it, and had now brought it to the very passable stage, yet had deeply envied, on a visit to a large hotel in

Philadelphia during the past winter, the seemingly effort-less ease with which staff there could marry the once-seen face to the once-heard name.

The major fault of the Brunel was that it was an up-mar-ket hotel in what had become a holiday resort for the poor and the elderly. The bulk of the local money was in the inland towns. The candy-floss trippers might well have had the money to eat or stay at the Brunel — they certainly spent almost as much in the seafront cafés which advertised *sardines sur toast* on their menus — but they were intimi-dated by the imposing proportions of the hotel. Maybe the Brunel was not so much like a misplaced dowager as a stranded whale.

It had been hard work to attain a reasonable occupancy rate over the year. In the first three months of the year espec-ially, Westercote could be a damp, deserted place. The musical weekends had been a highly successful innovation of his: a string quartet was invited down from the capital to give explanatory talks and perform, sometimes they'd even agree to a public rehearsal. At other times a couple of soloists from Welsh National Opera might come across the Channel, and the success of the season had been the St Valentine's Day programme of Victorian and Edwardian ballads. It was a good buy, £75 for three days including dinner, making the normal daily rate of £37.50 appear even more ludicrous than usual. Why couldn't we emulate the Americans or French, who could provide accommoda-tion which was equally good at half the price? Well, for a start we couldn't do it because of the British hotel worker's attitude towards service, and for seconds because the guests insisted on antiquated, expensive flummeries, such as morning tea and sandwiches in rooms late at night. The Americans had phased that out and the French had simply never entertained it.

'Good evening, Mrs Manners. Was it a good day's play?'

Kay Manners achieved the near-impossible, an attractive grimace.

'Very exciting, but you'll have heard that we lost, I suppose?'

'Yes. Rather a pity. We'd have had a high old time in the hotel tonight if the County had managed to pull it off.'

He escorted her to the lift. 'We may be quite busy in the dining-room later on just the same. I'd advise coming down not much later than eight-thirty.'

'Thanks, but I'm not all that hungry tonight. Too long a day in the sun, I think. I may have something light sent up later.'

'Certainly, just as you wish. The kitchens will be able to serve you until ten, as usual. Good evening.'

He broke off as Jenny Monteith went past towards the dining-room. That was a good-looking girl, that one, but she appeared angry and upset. Had it anything to do with the other night, he wondered, and forgot about it for the moment.

He looked in for a word with the hostess in the Isambard Lounge and the barman of the Kingdom Bar. The latter was giving his shelves a totally superfluous polish while waiting for custom to arrive. A small man with very bright eyes, his hair was anachronistic, centre-parted and oiled down, like a barber's trade magazine advertisement of half a century before.

'Ready for action stations, Mr Riordan.'

The manager nodded. 'You'll get off lighter than we hoped, Norrie. With the championship up the creek this place'll be like a bloody wake tonight.'

'I've always heard they shift plenty of the hard stuff at

those, Mr Riordan. Or am I wrong?'

'Norrie, you're not wrong. When I said wake I meant morgue.'

'Ah, they'll be in here to drown their sorrows and tell each other what they'll do next season.'

Riordan went back out to Reception. He liked to walk the whole hotel at least twice in the course of an evening. See and be seen, for the benefit of staff every bit as much as guests.

Cricket week was interesting. Because the Brunel was the only hotel in town worth the name, everyone tended to stay there, the County Committee, the quality Press, the visiting side, even one or two of the home players.

Dermot Riordan had played cricket at Belvedere College, Dublin, and had quite enjoyed it without ever in the least being captivated by it. He was glad he'd played, it meant that this week he could make sensible if facile conversation with a variety of people. He could argue about physical courage in sport with Sir Anthony, who maintained that facing really fast bowling was the ultimate test of sporting bravery, whereas he himself contended that the jumping horses were what tested a man to the limit. Though in truth the last time he'd been in his native Kilkenny he'd gone along to see the county hurlers, and he'd have to put them high up on any list.

The ritual of cricket week at Westercote appealed to him, pity it wasn't still a fortnight like the old days, the hotel could certainly have used the revenue. He thought this even in the satisfied consciousness that he'd done well by the Brunel — he was left in no doubt of that at his job scrutiny the previous month. 'We see a fine future for you, Mr Riordan, with us in the Antelope Hotel Group.'

It came down to gauging the clientele you had and were

likely to have. The Brunel moved at an amble. Take this week. Sunday morning was sitting in the glass-fronted terrace, reading and discarding the heavy Sundays for the light lunch that was prelude to the John Player League match. The Sunday evening could be slightly fraught since, of recent years, some undesirables had come back from the game to the hotel, attracted by the licensing hours and the very good and very cheap set dinner. But, after all, it was simply a matter of liaising with the *maitre d'hôtel*, encouraging him to size up the situation and express himself desolated that there were no tables available.

The regular guests, fairly staid, need not and should not be upset. In certain respects the hotel had moved with the times: it was quite a while since the God's Wonderful Railway Disco had joined the list of attractions, but it was as remotely located as possible. The image worked at was that of solid, fortyish, monied comfort, so that despite the existence of the GWR, young people who found themselves in the hotel tended to look around them in a kind of dazed disbelief. All during the last war the Brunel had provided safe haven against the winds of austerity and rationing for ladies of uncertain age and assured incomes.

The occasional Sunday night person apart, the cricketers posed few problems, unlike the rugby players. They had been compelled to refuse an Easter booking from a rugby team from Mountain Ash way. No amount of money spent by them at the bar could offset the damage to fixtures and fittings. The rugby boys had tried though, give them that, a phone call had come from a man purporting to be the secretary of the Inverness club, but since his accent was redolent of the valleys — good for Yvonne the receptionist who was on to it — he was told that there was no room at the inn.

Riordan watched the dining-room fill up and reflected that for sheer mindless destruction, the Dublin Horse Show crowd at the Shelburne would take some whacking. Beyond a certain point in the social scale, of course, loutish bad manners entered the realm of jolly japery and a mention in *The Tatler*. It was harder to see the funny side if you were a young chambermaid drenched by buckets of water, or a waiter whose face had been embedded in the sweet trolley.

No, he'd take the cricketers, a biddable bunch on the whole. There was the occasional flutter, of course, and the sight of the Monteith girl eating systematically on her own brought his mind back to the Mayor's Reception a couple of nights before. She hadn't been with that young cricketer — Pontefract, was it his name was? — that night, any more than she was tonight, yet for the rest of the time they'd seemed inseparable.

There had been a disco after His Worship had said his piece about what a joy it was to see the cricketers back again, and ties of friendship strengthened through sport, and all the rest of it. At the disco Frank Applegarth had been very chief with the girl, even allowing for the physical aloofness of disco dancing. Nor was that all. At three in the morning Mrs Trefusis in 316 had taken a bad turn and the doctor had been required to turn out. About an hour or so later he'd gone up just to make sure things were under control, and as he rounded a corner of the corridor, Applegarth emerged from 327, which was Jenny Monteith's room. No doubt at all of its being Applegarth, still less of its being 327 and, whatever he'd called up there for, it was certainly not to discuss the weather or the prospects for next spring's Gold Cup at Cheltenham.

Hotels were like that and it was none of his business. He

had no hankering for the days of the old-style American hotel where the job of the house-dick was to make sure that no non-resident set foot above ground level. Life was complicated enough without that. Riordan, a passably good-looking fellow, had experienced both his offers and his moments, which as an unmarried twenty-eight year old, he felt free to take up and enjoy. As his great friend Eamonn Keogh used to say, 'Derry, the wages of sin is death, but the fringe benefits are bloody marvellous.' Winter's traces were closing in though, last time home in Kilkenny his mother had spoken long and earnestly about the need to acquire a wife and settle down.

Applegarth and Jenny Monteith most certainly did not in any sense shock him, but it did surprise him. It was an odd attraction and the venue seemed unnecessarily perilous when a drive out along the cliff-tops would have been safer if draughtier.

A waiter brought him a note which he read and put in his pocket without reply. In a few moments Sir Anthony and Peter Latimer emerged from the dining-room and made their way through to the lounge for coffee.

'Sir Anthony?'

'Yes?'

'A message from Mr Constable in the Kingdom Bar. He says that if you've the inclination, he'd be very pleased if you'd join him for a nightcap.'

'Hm.' The President stood for a moment irresolute. 'I suppose it's the civil thing to do, Peter. Bit late in the evening, though, if he's going to give us a curtain lecture on the profligacy of the committee's ways.' He turned back to Riordan. 'Very good. You can say we'll join him in twenty minutes or so.' The same waiter was despatched with the news.

Hotel school, six months in Switzerland, the Shelburne, Parknasilla and, his first command, the Brunel. Ahead of him, the road had several interesting junctions. There was a case for going as assistant manager or relief manager to one of the chain's big London flagships. Or, since he was embarked upon a career where you carried your expertise without luggage, he should have a spell abroad. The six months in Switzerland had served to make his French functional, but it could stand improvement, and his German was kitchen-Deutsch, nothing more. Antelope Hotels would keep the tabs on him wherever he went.

The lobby seemed stuffy to him suddenly, and he went to the main door, breathing the sea air deeply before the heavy drops of rain began to spot his dinner-jacket. It was to be hoped the weather would clear for the Warwickshire game tomorrow, no percentage in having the potential matchgoers cooped up in the hotel all day. The bar would do rather more business but the staff would bear the brunt of the frustration and ill-temper occasioned by the weather.

He was on the point of going to the Kingdom Bar for the one drink he allowed himself with the guests when he saw the Monteith girl's man friend approaching. As he came through the revolving doors, Riordan noticed that his face was bruised and discoloured, and that despite the hour he wore dark glasses. He nodded in response to the manager's pleasant greeting but said nothing, going directly to the lifts.

Unhurriedly Dermot Riordan moved through the main ground floor corridor to the Kingdom Bar, his vigilant eye picking up an idling waiter here, a specially helpful receptionist there. Jenny Monteith was the kind of girl who could legitimately expect to have competition for her ... favours? Archaic. Hand? Probably something more interesting anatomically, if less permanent emotionally. Somehow, Pontefract didn't strike him as being quite the right name.

CHAPTER 13

The Overseas Player

Eleven years had passed since Rupert Delaval had been invited to come over to England for a trial season with the County, but the day on which the offer was made still stood bright and clear in the Antiguan's mind. Seventeen years of age, he had taken the new ball to open the bowling for his township of Old Road against a touring side from England, Trailblazers.

Trailblazers provided respectable opposition, including a former Test player of early nineteen fifties vintage, two University Blues, a couple of highly proficient club crick-eters and a youngster from MCC Ground Staff brought along to put flesh on otherwise rather emaciated bowling. The other players were of that variety whose money and availability, rather than any great playing skills, had found them places on the tour.

On the little ground at Old Road, within sight and sound of the sea, Rupert Delaval had roared in like an avenging angel, all high arm and spinnaker shirt. A Trailblazers' side which certainly batted down to a competent number seven was shot out on a hard, true wicket for a mortifying 83, and seven of their wickets toppled to Delaval for 29 runs, four of them without assistance. He was scarcely back in the dressing-room when Ken Lightbody was asking to see him.

Ken Lightbody ran the biggest haulage contractor's business in the county, and the County Cricket Club was his passion, monopolising all those hours in which he was not actually at business. Mrs Lightbody said feelingly that matters had reached the point where the purpose of running the haulage company was to keep the county club in existence. Her husband, a thickening, greying, but youthful looking man, might well have agreed with her. His hard work over the last eighteen months had earned him these three West Indian weeks. He hoped it might earn him also a few fours off the edge batting humbly at number nine, but most of all he hoped he might find a player for the County, preferably a fast bowler. Half an hour after seeing Delaval take the ball, he was convinced that he had found one.

As ever, he moved decisively. He persuaded their next opponents, in the island capital St John's, to let the youngster turn out for Trailblazers against them. Delaval bowled a little tensely, and another island youth with the imposing name of Isaac Vivian Alexander Richards got after him a bit, but he showed that he had real pace and, more importantly, that he could come back for a second spell. His contribution to the match was 4 for 79 and an uninhibited 27, going in just ahead of Lightbody. In addition, he sped effortlessly and like lightning around the boundary and threw the ball in like a shell. It was enough. It was more than enough.

Bowler and tour organiser had talked things over quietly in St John's Cathedral of all places, the breeze blowing coolly through the open doors and stirring the tattered

121

standards which recalled long-disbanded regiments in garrison. Below them memorial tablets commemorated innumerable subalterns who had found yellow fever a more potent adversary than Frenchman or Spaniard.

There followed a return visit to Old Road where Rupert's father rightly took some convincing that his son's welfare would be looked after.

'It's a very uncertain game, Mr Lightbody.'

'Indeed, Mr Delaval. I'd never seek to deny it. But a lot of fellows from West Indies have been very successful in our first class game. And very popular too. The crowds and the members love them.'

Delaval's father looked at him directly. 'And off the field? Are they loved there as well?'

Lightbody considered. 'I think I can honestly tell you that in my experience, the most important thing there is the player's personality. I'd be lying if I said there might not be problems. He's bound to miss all this.' He gestured expansively at the small garden, beyond whose neatness the long waves rolled lazily to the beach.

'Will your people do anything for him outside cricket?'

Lightbody smiled at him in a satisfied way. 'It won't be up to them. I'll pay the cost of bringing Rupert over. If he can drive — I forgot to ask him that by the way — he can have a job with my business any time he's available. Though I'd rather he went to technical college or something like that. He seems a bright lad.'

'He has his School Certificate,' the other said proudly, 'and he can drive. I drive the bus between here and St John's, it's a little twenty-seater Mercedes, and Rupert has quite often stood in for me.'

So it was settled. The youngster was called in to hear of his father's approval. Already there was something of leave-taking in his eyes as he glanced around the spotless, ordinary little room.

'Goodbye, Mr Delaval,' Lightbody said, shaking hands. 'Thank you for entrusting your son to us. We'll see that he keeps out of bother, Mrs Delaval,' — this to the mother who was standing nervously beside her boy. 'We'll find a nice family for him to stay with. Goodbye, Rupert, you can expect to hear from us in a couple of weeks.'

He had heard, and the family selected for him, Tim and Kay Manners, had kept him in England during that dismal first spring and summer of his qualification. It was difficult to adjust to the ragbag of matches that he played in, decent club matches at the weekend, minor counties and Second Eleven in midweek, with the occasional fill-in for Club and Ground scratch sides.

Tim chatted with him, Kay fed him and mothered him, and if there was any supervision it was of the gentlest kind. They included him in their cinema-going and visiting, although he suspected that some of their friends found it an odd situation. He accepted every other invitation, but on numerous occasions would say that he had somewhere to go, although that somewhere was a perambulation of the county town from one end to the other. Before he had been there two months he could have passed an examination for professional guide. He even found himself memorising the patterns of the lace curtains on the windows of the little red houses which marched in dreary, right-angled rows from the main street. For the rest of his life he would hear his own footsteps echoing in his ears as he trudged those streets in the long grey evening light that was so alien to him.

Occasionally he drove lorries for Ken Lightbody's firm and did odd jobs around the county ground. It took him fully a year to win anything approaching acceptance but, fortunately, he had the good sense to realise that his colour was only the additional factor. The facts of life in first class cricket were that in the English game, there was room for around three hundred players, no more. In such a fiercely competitive business a newcomer to the staff was a potential threat to one's livelihood, no matter if he came from Antigua or Accrington.

Midway through his first season he was on the point of flying home but was dissuaded by a firm phone call from Old Road, which Kay had instigated although he never knew it. His chance came at the beginning of his second year, when Freddy Bond, who'd bowled fast medium for getting on for fourteen seasons, sustained the back injury in the first championship match which was to finish his career. A late phone call to the Manners' house told him to be at Northampton for ten next morning, and Kay was up at crack of dawn to drive him.

At lunchtime, after eighty minutes of play punctuated by sleety squalls, his figures were 9-1-41-0. He had bowled abysmally, three wides and four no-balls were due to be added to that total, and he had become increasingly despondent as he banged the ball into a pudding of a wicket. The captain, Paul Day, offered him no advice whatever, merely managing a 'Thank you, Rupert' between compressed lips. Thanks mainly to the youngster's undisciplined bowling, Northants were enjoying lunch at 82 for 0.

He collected his ludicrously inappropriate salad and took it back to the dressing-room where, swathed in three sweaters, he picked at it dispiritedly. The rest of the side were in the players' dining-room, swapping reminiscence and off-colour jokes with old acquaintances. Delaval looked out of the windows where the flags stood out

124

straight under grey, scurrying clouds. It was one thing to knock over a few wickets when the opposition was second-rate and the sun was on your back. The Northants openers had played him this morning with all the time in the world, played him as if he were a slow bowler and a poor one at that.

'You don't *look* stupid.'

He raised his eyes, startled. Frank Applegarth stood in the doorway regarding him unsmilingly.

'I'm sorry?'

'I said, you don't *look* stupid.' He came into the dressing-room and closed the door. 'So why do you bowl stupid?'

Rupert felt himself kindling despite the fact that he knew he'd been dreadful in the morning session.

'I'm sorry,' he said again, stiffly. 'I assure you I'm trying my hardest.'

'You're trying a bloody sight too hard.'

'Isn't that the idea?'

'Look, this isn't one of your cast iron tracks in Antigua. You're a big strong lad, but you can't bowl with shoulders and arms on this blancmange of a wicket. So for Christ's sake try using your brains.'

'Cut down on pace, you mean?'

'I knew you didn't look stupid. Length and line, sun-shine, that's it. Put the ball up there and let late movement do the rest. Pitch it in short like you've been doing and you might just as well throw it to the boundary yourself. Geoff Cook had time to comb his hair before hooking you over mid-wicket. Note that, sunshine, over *mid*-wicket.'

Delaval somehow felt a little more cheerful. 'Thank you. I'll give it a try. If I ever get on again, that is.'

'You will. I'll have a word with the skipper about it. If he was worth a damn he'd have told you this, not me. Remember, off stump and just outside.'

It was late in the afternoon before the Antiguan was grudgingly recalled by Paul Day. His first over was a tentative and fortunate maiden, but a maiden it was. In his second spell, gaining in confidence, he took 3 for 20 and that, with a quick 29 in the second innings which made the match safe, was enough to keep him in the side.

He had rarely been out of it since, except for the season when the County in an excess of zeal had recruited a Tasmanian opener and the Natal wicket-keeper. His own appearances were therefore severely limited because of the restrictions on overseas players, but fortunately the South African had decided after that one year that Pietermaritzburg was infinitely preferable to Westercote.

Over the years he had slowed down a bit, although given the right wicket he could still make the ball climb uncomfortably for five overs or so. It was disappointing that he seldom got the chance to bat seriously, only on a Sunday did the opportunity arise to go in as high as number seven. He'd notched a few half centuries in the Championship, usually in the night watchman situation, but he'd taken in the last year to batting in glasses, and he could see that his future lay as an uninhibited tail-ender who might get you thirty or more probably go first or second ball.

From his start as a boy from Old Road, he'd managed nine years as a county cricketer, never considered by West Indies for Tests but with six hundred wickets in first-class cricket and with a benefit due year after next, following Frank's testimonial.

He owed a lot to Frank. Applegarth was never effusive, was never particularly polite, but he had been a good friend. His was the first invitation home from a fellow-player, and no season went by without Rupert spending three or four evenings with Frank and Alice. They had made Tilly feel very welcome too, precisely because there had been no fanfare of trumpets, no stultifying preparations.

Applegarth had courted trouble for him at an early stage in his career. Delaval had put down a very takeable catch at long-on and the Cambridge vice-captain, who was in the County side, had drawled, 'Stir yourself, choc-ice, there's a good fellow.' Applegarth looked at his captain and the speaker. When, a few balls later, Rupert, with a brilliant stoop and return, turned a four into a single, the Light Blue's voice rose again, this time in approbation. 'Well fielded, choc-ice!'

He was shaken as Applegarth drifted over to him as they crossed in the field. 'You're still at college, sonny, so it's obvious you've got things to learn. Now learn this. You call Delaval that once again and I'll boot your fucking arse all around this ground. And I won't wait for the tea interval to do it.' He moved away expressionlessly.

Today, after hundreds of matches together, they had been in sight of the championship, and for Frank, of the all-time batting record. How had it slipped? He would have bet his plane fare to Antigua that Applegarth would have won the match without even requiring six and seven to come in. Over years of watching him he had come to know with great accuracy when he was in form or not. Today he had been in prime form, never forced into the hurried shot, the runs mounting as the inexorable placements went on, eliminating risk. Then a run-out that would have earned twelve-year-olds a ticking off. Yet, certainly, it had looked a sure run.

With a little less impetuosity he himself might just have retrieved matters. He was seeing the ball well then, trying to drive over the bowler's head, he found that Ezra Moseley had dropped it that little bit short, he drove without quite getting there, and mid-off took a spectacular but not especially taxing catch.

Palfreyman hadn't done much but that wasn't surprising, he'd be very remorseful at having been at least partly the cause of Frank losing his wicket. It was a great pity about the Championship, and an even greater pity about the nine centuries. He must be careful not to say that to anybody, team performance came first. But there would be many other years for the County, whereas Frank would not know another summer such as this.

His senior colleague would need his sympathy but not now. He began to think of his coming return to Antigua where he would spend the winter coaching, and with luck might manage to be selected for a couple of matches for the Leewards in the Shell Shield. It was almost too early to start thinking about his own benefit, year after next. He'd need an attractive benefit tie, some combination of the West Indian background and County emblem.

He hoped and thought the benefit would go quite well. He wasn't a Viv, of course, but there was only one of them, thank God, for there was just nowhere you could bowl to him if he decided to get after you. Being a run of the mill county cricketer could work quite well for you at benefit time, you'd played much more often than the Test boys, and there was often a feeling amongst members that the faithful packhorse should be rewarded. Maybe Viv could be persuaded to bring a team down to play in one of his benefit Sunday matches?

In a suprisingly cheerful frame of mind he waved Kay Manners out of the ground, missing Tim as he did so, and went in search of Tilly.

CHAPTER 14

The Beer Tent Lady

Joyce Tattersall was every bit as much a part of Westercote Week as the teams, scorers, ground staff or the double-decker bus that did duty as the ladies' loo. In the middle forties and of middle height, she had a hard-won slimness. No one could deny that she was an attractive woman, even if the make-up was a little dramatic, the hair remorselessly in place. In the 'sixties it would have been lacquered beyond endurance.

She dressed neatly and unfussily, her overall was spotless, and while there was a faint suggestion of the common about her, it nevertheless seemed strange that she could preside over the beer tent in cricket week. She was an experienced president too, for she had been doing it since she was a young woman in her late twenties. The great tent had blown down around her in the dreadful gale of 1968 when a falling crate had knocked her out, while a mere eight years afterwards the trodden white grass of the floor had been covered with sunstroke victims dragged out of the stifling heat.

By the nature of things she saw very little of the cricket,

and felt not in the slightest deprived by this. As a game it was all right, she supposed, but hardly to be compared with soccer. The customers liked to talk about the game, however, and she had learned over the years to organise her own information service so that she could make intelligent noises.

Some of the customers, the nicer ones, liked to talk about the game. Some of them were after the other. Usually it was goodhumoured enough, somebody like old Mr Hardcastle (there was an inappropriate name) would say as he grasped his pint, 'I thought you and I might go down the beach tonight, Joyce.'

'Sorry, love, you're not nearly strong enough!'

If they came on a bit heavier than that, then a couple of well-placed Anglo-Saxons could work wonders. There were times, even at that, when the swinging right hand to the chops was the only reliable deterrent. Bernie Masterton had found that out one day when he'd come in very early in the morning to the tent while she was half way up a ladder hammering nails into the tent pole. As she felt his hand go under her skirt she lashed out with her heel before inviting him to explain to his wife the exact circumstances in which he had come by the weal on his face.

On the whole, during the week, you were dealing with nice people. Sunday was an entirely different matter, fighting off shirtless, beer-bellied idiots whose party piece was to climb on the outside to the very apex of the tent and then slide down the canvas. Regrettably, everyone who had tried this had avoided serious injury.

Things were a little better at the John Player games now because, two years ago, the entire bar staff had said they would refuse to crew the tent on Sundays unless some action was taken. So now there were usually two or three policemen hovering around, and the bar didn't open until half-past four. The yobbos could still bring their own though. The Somerset supporters were the worst of the lot, trying to live up to their reputation as lovable yokels and failing miserably, ignorant clodhoppers they were. Thank God next year's JPL was at Taunton, as good as a rise, was that.

Business was steady in the tent, even given the excitement generated by what looked like a successful run-chase against Glamorgan. They never got the beer queue down below a dozen, or the tea line to less than six. When the news of Applegarth's fall was conveyed to Joyce by woebegone members, she steadied herself for action. She might mutter 'Too bad!', 'What a shame!', 'He will be disappointed', and a dozen other useful variants to those regulars who crowded in at the fall of his, and subsequent wickets. For Applegarth, however, she felt nothing at all. Another fellow who couldn't keep his hands to himself, and he seemed to think that her staff had nothing else to do than dance attendance on him and the other players at lunchtime. That wasn't where the profit came from, she could tell him.

It was no coincidence that the people who were obviously used to better things, such as Sir Anthony and Mr Latimer, were so much easier to deal with. She realised now what her father had meant when he said, 'You'll find that money's better being at the top, girl.'

She came abruptly out of her daydream. 'Doris!'

'Yes, Miz Tattersall?'

'Look out at the field. Who's batting?'

'Rupert and that Mr Palfreyman.' In the same breath, 'Hold on, Rupert's out.'

'Right. It looks like we'll lose. Get on the phone to Partridge's and tell them to halve the number of pasties, pies and filled rolls for tomorrow. Let me know when you've done, I'll want to get on to the brewers. Forecast's for rain tomorrow, anyway, shouldn't think we'll get a full day's play, and even if we do, the crowd'll be down a good bit if we lose today.'

Bar takings were subtly linked to the weather. A cold spell was bad, although obviously you sold more tea and coffee. Persistent rain was ruinous because people simply left the ground. The ideal was a very hot day with a short heavy shower about three, which would fill the tent for an hour or so but pose no serious threat to the resumption of play.

The slurred 'Miz Tattersall' of Doris reflected the general ambivalence regarding Joyce's marital status. She habitually wore a wedding ring, but nobody had ever seen a Mr Tattersall, nor ascertained whether she was really a Mrs Mainwaring or Phipps or whatever. There was a feeling that perhaps widowhood had embraced her, and for all her bawdy repartee in the beer tent, she was not seen around Westercote with anyone and played no favourites. Tilly Dempster knew the truth of the situation, which was that the beer tent manageress *was* Mrs Joyce Tattersall, whose marriage to a merchant seaman, Roy Tattersall, had ended in the divorce courts a long time ago. Joyce was her aunt, and between the two a considerable affection existed. It was to the older woman that Tilly's mother had, three months since, assigned the task of undoing, if possible, the girl's engagement to Rupert Delaval.

'I don't want to do that, Maureen,' Joyce said firmly to her sister. 'He's a nice lad, I see him at the ground and, believe me, he's a damn sight better than some of our people. Anyhow, Tilly's a grown woman at twenty-three.

She has to be allowed to choose for herself.'

'All I want you to do is talk to her.'

'No, Maureen. What you want me to do is to come back and tell you that I've worked the oracle and that it's all off. Tilly marries the boy next door, general rejoicing, and final dance of the loyal peasants.'

Tilly's mother shook her head, bewildered and unhappy. 'I've nothing at all against Rupert. He's a thoroughly nice boy and he worships Tilly, but I want to be sure she's thought it out. Where will they live? What will he do, eventually? What if they have any children? I don't want to run her life, she's twenty-three as you say, but I need to feel satisfied that she's aware of all the pitfalls.'

Reluctantly, therefore, Joyce talked to her niece, feeling a very indirect responsibility for the situation in that the two had met three years ago when Tilly, during her annual holidays from teacher training college, had helped out in the beer tent during Westercote Week.

Tilly stood decidedly before her in Joyce's flat in Cheltenham, not sullen but with a settled obstinacy. She was taller than her aunt, her brown hair cut short and straight, her skin agreeably freckled. Only her eyes, quizzical and aware, were at all remarkable, she was otherwise simply a pleasant-looking girl.

'It won't work, Aunt Joyce.'

'I'm not out to make anything work or not work. Please don't "Aunt Joyce" me, it's enough of an ordeal to face the mirror every day. "Joyce" will do perfectly well enough.'

'Very well then,' — avoiding the name. 'Rupert and I will marry. When the season ends.'

'Your mother is anxious that you've thought it all out.'

'I don't know how she can say that. We've talked it over, dozens of times.'

'Do you think she likes Rupert?'

'She says she does. I believe she really does. She likes him better than she did Gerry Lazenby.'

Joyce Tattersall lit a cigarette and frowned. 'It's almost certainly not you, nor Rupert, nor family. It's how the people you meet will react. Can you cope with that?'

'I don't know. It will be very difficult.'

'It will be *very* difficult. People can be hideously cruel, malicious, destructive. Have you any idea of the things they are liable to say?'

'Yes.' The answer was unequivocal, unvarnished.

'How can you possibly know?'

'Rupert has told me. He's had a lot of experience. He's coached me in every insult they will fling, every phone call they might make.'

'It's an odd way to conduct a courtship.'

'In our position it's a very sensible way. Rupert says that he would never marry me unless I know *exactly* how it will be, the filthy taunts, the abuse — not prettied up but spelled out.'

'What about future plans?'

'Rupert has his benefit year after next. After that he reckons he's got perhaps another two seasons in county cricket. We can't really think beyond that yet.'

They moved into the kitchen, still talking. 'If you get married, might it affect his position with the County?'

'Why should it? There are quite a few mixed marriages involving county players, according to Rupert. I'm quite sure some of the team might not like it. Sometimes the ones who smile and chat are the ones who will cause most mischief.'

Her aunt blew smoke through her nose and looked directly at Tilly.

'What have you decided about children?'

'We will welcome them if and when they come.'

'Far harder for the children.'

'Yes. Petted when they're young, told they're "adorable". Great favourites at school, then when they're twelve or so, they'll start to get left out.'

'Your Rupert seems to be very perceptive.'

Tilly smiled. 'He is. But what I've just told you I've also discussed with Kay Manners, Rupert's landlady.'

'Supposing Rupert found that he could get work back in the West Indies. How could you settle on Antigua? I hear it's tiny.'

'It is, Aunt Joyce.' She held up a hand in apology. 'Sorry. Well, I can't say till I've seen it, which will be next month. There's very little work out there though. He'd have rather more choice here.'

'More coffee?'

'Fine.'

'Your mother, we both know this, is worried stiff because you are set on marrying across the colour line. That's a very natural thing, Tilly, you mustn't be angry with her.'

'Honestly . . . Joyce . . . I'm not at all angry with her.'

'It'd maybe be different if there weren't just the two of you. But it should be a happy occasion when a daughter marries.'

'Were your parents happy, Aunt Joyce?'

'Very.' She smiled grimly. 'And it turned out marvellously, I don't think.'

'Rupert's parents aren't very happy.'

'I'm surprised to hear that.'

'Promotion for their son, why should they be unhappy? They don't see it like that. Rupert says they've spent the last two summers throwing every unmarried girl in Old Road at his head.'

'And that doesn't worry you?'

'Of course. He's a handsome devil, quite distinguished with the glasses now when he goes out to bat, isn't he? No, his parents must be worried, as Mum is. It's my job to convince them that I'll make him a good wife.'

There was a rock-like simplicity in the girl which deeply affected Joyce.

'From my heart out, Tilly, I hope things work out better for the two of you than they did with me. It's just that marriage is damned hard anyhow, even without additional complications. Lots of money could help your situation, but you haven't got that.'

Tilly shook her head calmly. 'No, or at any rate not yet. Pray for a good summer two years on and that Rupert's in bowling form. You'll buy a benefit tie?'

'Half-a-dozen. I'll wear no other.'

She had gone back to Maureen and advised her to prepare for a wedding with Tilly's parting words in her mind. 'Rupert has told me that people will let you down badly and hurt you badly, but you must keep the ability to be hurt. "They all lived happily every after" won't happen. I know he's right, and I'm prepared to try to see that *we* live happily most of the time.'

Outside the beer tent it had started to rain and the first drops spotted softly against the canvas. Joyce shot a glance at the clock which showed fifty-six minutes after stumps.

'Five minutes till closing, drink up, lads, if you please. *If* you please, Harry' — to a youth who had removed his shirt and was inflicting gyrating movements on his pelvis which would surely be damaging in the long term.

Without malice, the lad struck a suggestive pose and

grinned.

'Fancy a night with a ten stone bundle of dynamite, Joyce?'

'Not if it's got a three inch fuse,' and the discomfited Harry to his eternal credit joined in the general laughter. The tent was tidied, the empties stacked, the litter cleared away. Quickly and deftly she cashed up. Jackie, the head lad, saw her off the premises.

'Takings were good today, Miz Tattersall.'

'Very fair. We've had the best of the week though, Jackie, it's not shaping well for tomorrow.'

'No, it's not. Pity about the game today. I'd have liked to see old Frank get his nine tons.'

'All you're supposed to see, m'lad, is the ale pouring into the customers' glasses.'

'I mean "see" in a manner of speaking. Shouldn't suppose he'll manage it now.'

'He's got two games left,' his boss said indifferently. 'What is it Sir Anthony's always on about in the lunch tent, "the glorious uncertainty of cricket"?'

Jackie went off up town on foot while Joyce Tattersall prepared to drive back to Cheltenham. On an impulse she stopped her car on the sea front, despite the increasingly gloomy drizzle. Beyond the two islands a coaster was making its way sedately south. She thought of the little island to which her niece would go, and of the merchant seaman who had been her husband. For a minute or so she sat in dry-eyed regret for a sense of waste, rather than of loss. Then she started up the car again and hoped that she'd got the calculations right for tomorrow's feeding and watering.

CHAPTER 15

The County Treasurer

There are some people whose occupation or profession seems greatly to be at odds with their appearance. Eric Constable was not one of those. Very small, tiny really, fastidiously neat, his cautious manner of speaking and considered air of reserve proclaimed the accountant that he had been before taking an early retirement three years previously.

In one respect he was deceptive. He was almost yellow-skinned, and this, with his oily, glossy hair and bandbox smartness, made the observer think of a Gurkha or Malay soldier. Constable, however, was totally lacking in military background, since even National Service had been ruled out for him by the discovery of a shadow on one of his lungs.

His devotion was not so much to cricket itself as to keeping the County club in existence. He had therefore seen the run-out without feeling anything, though quite convinced of the correctness of Applegarth's dismissal. No regret, annoyance, anger or despair racked his soul. While he watched detachedly, his mind was elsewhere — on next year's balance sheet, on the financial prospects for the season after that.

Supporters there were in abundance, fund-raisers too for that matter, but long-term solvency was the concern of a very few. Most members saw no further than the annual subscription, though there were exceptions; that Scotch chap the other day had demonstrated a remarkable grasp of what was required to keep a first-class cricket club going these days.

Cricket was almost as expensive as opera and, strictly speaking, made as little financial sense. People were always bleating about running the game on businesslike lines. He liked to think he'd done quite a lot in that direction, but would cheerfully have admitted that the most business-like thing any of the seventeen first-class counties could do would be to pass a motion of dissolution.

If he felt anything at all about the run-out it was a flicker of irritation towards Applegarth. Had Glamorgan been defeated it would have meant a bumper crowd for the three days of the Warwick match, and that, with subsequent prize money, could have gone quite a bit towards bringing out the season on the right side.

The figures for the current season lay littered across the bed of his room at the Brunel. Not too bad, in many respects; they'd only lost one home JPL to rain and the three-day attendances were up, however slightly, very few counties could say that. But . . .

His reservations were interrupted by a tap on the door. 'Come in.'

A waiter came in, carrying a heavy tray, closing the door awkwardly with his hip.

'Just set it down on the dressing table, will you? I'd put it back a few inches' — the 'a' in back broad enough to hint at his Hereford boyhood. 'Thanks. Here you are.' He gave the waiter a fifty pence tip.

'Thank you, sir. That's one round of beef, one of cheese and tomato, as ordered. Will that be everything? Then goodnight, sir,' in response to Constable's nod. He went out, swerving dexterously round the child-sized shoes that lay between dressing table and door.

The treasurer poured some tea into a cup, refilling the teapot from the water jug. His lips moved soundlessly as he staked out his battle lines for the impending meeting with Sir Anthony and the executive. He had fought this particular campaign before and lost, twice, but the County was going to have to listen to him this time — or conceivably go under in three-four years. He could, even at this stage, predict Sir Anthony's deflecting response.

'The members'll never stand for it, Eric. The County have been playing at Westercote since 1907. Damn it, I saw my first match here in 1923, when old Harry Bridges made 62 on one leg in our second knock. And anyway, we get our best gates here, far and away. Even you would have to admit that, you dedicated calculating machine!'

'Dessicated.'

'What's that?'

'Dessicated. I thought you were quoting.' He glided on. 'It's quite true that we pull in more people through the gate here than at the County ground, or Deignton for that matter, but that's only half the story. Almost all our additional revenue from here goes on tentage and on temporary stands. We have to detach the groundsman for a fortnight at the height of the summer. And I'll remind you that last year we opened a marvellous new pavilion at the County ground not thirty miles down the road. As I remember, it cost us half a million. In my submission, it's badly under-used.'

The President splayed his fingers across his left cheek in a Churchillian V, as was his habit when pondering.

'I don't know, Eric, we're a County club, not a town club. We've obligations to our members all over the shire. What's wrong with that? When I started here we played on six grounds every season, the three we've got plus Norton Florey, Lidding and Chapel Iseult.'

'I've seen the accounts book for that season,' said Constable, clinically unmoved. 'Most games there were six amateurs in the side, three of whom, yourself included, didn't even claim expenses.'

Sir Anthony, slightly out of his depth, struck out manfully.

'I've seen the accounts for *last* season. Seems to me we've rarely been better off in the last twenty years.'

'I agree. I'll go further, Sir Anthony. We've *never* been better off in the last twenty years, but cricket's like that. All we need is a wet Westercote and, with India the touring side next year, Test receipts will be well down, depend on it.'

That would be his line of attack. He poured himself some more tea and ate a sandwich absently, his mood as black as the late summer skies outside. His time, he knew, was not yet. There were other developments that bothered him. Applegarth was coming to the end of the road, and that could be a factor. He didn't put hundreds on the gate like a Richards or Botham, but he had his adherents, and Constable suspected that when he retired the county would lose more often.

There was no way of making money in the long term from County cricket. Somerset were coining it just now, but in a couple of years Richards and Garner would go,

141

three more might see Botham depart, and what then? The layman didn't realise either that the careful treasurer dreaded the successful year almost as much as the disastrous. On the basis of success achieved, pay deals were reached which seldom saw the triumphs of the previous season repeated.

Constable sighed wearily. He had a sense of humour, he was kind to animals and courteous to members. It was dispiriting to have to appear so frequently in the role of Mr Misery. At committee meetings, when captain and secretary would joyously announce plans for the awarding of someone's county cap during a tea interval of the next home match, he as treasurer had to qualify his approval of the doubtless well-earned honour by remarking that the Committee would of course have observed that this now brought the number of capped players to ten and that the financial implications of this would not have escaped them.

Capped players received benefits, and benefits induced the spirit of competition. Three years from now, no player was due a benefit, and this would be another revolutionary proposal he would lay before the committee — in that year the beneficiary should be the County club itself.

Applegarth was worth his testimonial, unlikeable and tight-fisted though he was. (Constable, when not operating as treasurer, was open-handed, although never foolishly so.) The veteran cricketer had two great qualities. He was a trier, invariably giving value for money, and he kept himself in excellent physical condition. Over the years Constable had groaned in impotent fury at highly-paid fast bowlers, almost every manjack of them a member in good standing of the Hypochondriacs' Union, who frequently felt the need to nurse a bruised heel or a taut hamstring. Only long rest, or the tip-off that a Selector was on the ground, held out any possibility of betterment for them.

His thoughts turned towards what little he had gathered of today's scuffle. Sir Anthony and Peter Latimer had been pretty unforthcoming — the President indeed had seemed to wish he could call back the few sketchy details he had given. Frank Applegarth could be very carnaptious when he'd a mind. If what he'd heard was true, it seemed a terrible thing to do to a young cricketer making his way.

The treasurer rather liked Richard Palfreyman, a frank, open young fellow, even if he did have a great deal to learn. Future county captain there, very possibly, though he'd have to start playing a few more strokes to guarantee his place in the side. Constable had a hunch that eventually his bowling might be his more useful weapon. His off-spin was far too prodigal for the limited over stuff, but he did turn the ball very markedly and could prove useful in a situation where the County had runs on the board and could afford to buy wickets.

That, however, was in the future and the proper concern of the cricket committee. He shuffled his papers together and yawned, looking at his watch. His own day was not quite over. He lifted the phone, asked for an outside line from the hotel switchboard, and dialled a Deignton number.

'Howard? Eric. Yes, we never sleep — nor should you marketing executives. Well, give me a moment and I'll tell you what I'm on about. I got a buzz today that Allardyce's may not underwrite the Festival here next year. The company's going through a bad patch and is looking to retrench. Any alternative thoughts? Unofficially, of course, at this stage,' he added hurriedly.

For the next few minutes they exchanged ideas, none of them particularly promising at first hearing.

'Blackadder's? It's a thought, Howard, but I don't know that they've ever given any indication of being particularly sports-minded.'

'Good PR, Eric, to give a helping hand to one of the oldest sporting institutions in their locality. I suppose, if no one emerges, we could always stick a couple of quid on the subscription.'

'I'd rather avoid that if I can,' the treasurer said cautiously. 'We've put subs up by forty per cent over the last three years and we're forever rattling collection pails in front of them on the ground itself. We may have overdone the Vice-President thing too, ordinary members are a bit miffed about that.'

'Why should they be? VP's pay three times as much, damn it!'

'I know, but a lot of people who've been members for years and can't look at the VP rate feel they're being squeezed out. I've a certain sympathy for them.'

'You're all heart, Mr Treasurer. What's the weather like down your end?'

'Same as yours, I imagine. High wind, heavy rain, abysmal.'

'Hm. Prospects of play tomorrow, would you say?'

'We might get some. I don't think there's any chance of a prompt start, barring miracles.'

'I was going to bring down another three or four dozen crested sweaters to sell from the shop. Maybe it's not a good idea.'

'There will be better days, I fancy. Oh, Howard . . .'

'Yes?'

'We'll be having the raffle at Christmas, I take it?'

'Absolutely. Matter of fact I tied up the first prize today, an afternoon flight for two in Concorde on one of its promotional trips.'

'That's not at all bad, Howard. I may even have a judicious speculation on that.'

'We aim to please. By the way, do we have a pluvius policy on this week?'

'Not any more. We used to, but the premium has become prohibitive. Of course, if we couldn't attract a sponsor next year, we'd certainly have to think hard.'

The voice at the other end said, 'In a minute, Kathleen.'

'Fine, Howard, I can take a hint.'

'Well, you see, Eric, we've got into this odd habit of having supper. By the way, what did you make of the fracas between Frank and young Dicky Palfreyman?'

'I didn't know there had been a fracas.'

'Pull the other one.'

'A difference of opinion is how I'd describe it, over the assignment of blame for a run-out. Strong words exchanged, no doubt, in the heat of the moment.'

'I hear that more than words were exchanged.'

'You do astonish me, Howard. It'll sort itself out, you'll see. Go and have your supper and keep me posted on the raffle.'

'It never ends,' his colleague said ruefully. 'It's like bailing out a leaky rowing-boat with a colander.'

'A forceful piece of imagery, and apt. I sometimes compare my own task to that of Sisyphus.'

'Sissy who?'

'Sisyphus. He was condemned eternally to push a huge stone to the top of a hill whence, on arrival, the stone rolled back down to the foot. You, being younger, of course, would miss out on our classical heritage. G'night, Howard.'

He went into the bathroom where he washed his face

and brushed his teeth. Howard Kirby was a good chap, he was hard-working, imaginative — that Concorde trip was a nice touch — and he generated a lot of revenue for the club. Some of the less intelligent players, such as Bernie Masterton and the opener, Charlie Cullis, were vitriolic in their criticisms of highly-paid chiefs, but the fact was that without the work of someone like Howard, those two would be grubbing around for a Birmingham League club that might employ them on a match basis.

He closed the door of his room and pocketed the key, feeling able to enjoy the promised drink with president and captain in the Kingdom Bar. On the way down in the lift he exchanged pleasantries with the manager, Constable having a regard for the Shelburne which went back to the first time he'd ever gone to a rugby international at Lansdowne Road. If time and place ever permitted, he'd like to ask Riordan about the financial mechanics of keeping a great barn of a place like this open all year. It was tempting to say it was all about survival nowadays, but it had always been so, the crises were there in the old Minute Books to prove it.

Crisis was the norm, he thought, as he stepped through the door of the bar, but he would not be telling that to Sir Anthony and company next Wednesday.

CHAPTER 16

The Girl Friend

Jenny Monteith closed the door of her hotel room noiselessly. There was no sound on the other side either, for Applegarth's footfalls were silent on the thickly carpeted corridor. She stood leaning against the door, face burning, at a loss to explain to herself what had happened.

She regarded herself as a liberated miss, so liberated that she bestowed very little thought on it. A 'sixties childhood and a 'seventies girlhood had given her a considerable freedom, even allowing for a fairly conventional Highgate schooling and middle-class North London upbringing. Two sisters and her mother had made the family home predominantly feminine, her father accepting majority rule with a graceful good humour which betokened considerable self-confidence.

She knew her first boy, in the biblical sense, while still a sixth former, and there had been others — two, therefore the plural — during her years at London University, by way of prelude to Vicente. Vicente of Vigo, a sinfully good-looking medical, had illumined Jenny's year in Spain as a language student. They had spent every spare moment, waking and sleeping, together, and their friendship had initially survived her return to England. Indeed, she had gone back to Vigo on holiday six months later, and for a couple of weeks the affair was as ardent as ever. Then gradually the letters became fewer, the answers more difficult and more stilted, the phrases absurdly formal, so that the eventual cessation of the correspondence was a matter for a measure of regret, but infinitely more an occasion of relief. In moments of sentiment and nostalgia she could picture once more Vicente and herself at the Yacht Club, looking out to the long, dark *rias* of Galicia or across to the houses of the city as they struggled up the hills. It was very evocative, and quite over.

Her meeting with Richard Palfreyman had come at a time when she was dissatisfied with her professional and personal life. A degree in languages and business methods had got her a job with a large wine importer in the City, but the prospect dangled at the interview of visits to French vineyards and the great Anglo-Hispanic sherry families had proved to be delusory. Six months in the job was enough to make plain to her that purely secretarial skills had won the position. Her linguistic talents would begin with 'Estimado Señor' and end on 'Su Seguro Servidor.' The job was dreary beyond description but not ill-paid, her salary was in fact such as to preclude any thought of leaving on a whim.

Vicente had not been replaced by anyone; his last letter, and it would be the *last* letter, had come to her four months ago. She agreed to go with Donna, her younger sister, to a party on the night before Christmas Eve without any great keenness. The crowd were likely to be slightly younger than she was, twenty-year olds possibly, and the venue did not particularly attract her. She couldn't exactly place

Thurloe Square, but if it was South Kensington then that meant traipsing across London. They'd gone by Tube, she remembered, and in sullen silence too. She had commandeered a top of Donna's or perhaps it had been the other way round, and this had caused friction.

She had gone home from the party — a good party — not with Donna, but with Richard Palfreyman. Donna was doing pretty well with a young naval sublieutenant and was quite happy to fall in with this arrangement, happier perhaps than Jenny herself initially was with her escort.

The boy was all right, quite good-looking in a blond, bland way, very good-looking in fact at first glance, until you saw that it was the fair wavy hair that did it, the features lacked any real distinction. Very anxious to let you know about his achievements, Geography graduate from Reading, or he would be in a few months' time, and had already played for the County, having been spotted with Berkshire. It was fashionable among Jenny's friends to despise athletes: 'Preserve me from a brainless jock!' was their cry. She was, therefore, less impressed than he would have wished.

Richard Palfreyman wasn't brainless, nor did he possess the unworldly cleverness of the true academic. He had a strong streak of practicality which emerged when he talked about his future career. The subject had come up as they left the house in Thurloe Square in search of a taxi, pausing occasionally to admire the restraint of the furniture and decorations of the lit drawing-rooms of the neighbouring houses. The night was lovely — starry, still, unseasonably mild. Jenny had been enlarging on the limitations of her job while Palfreyman listened sympathetically and attentively enough but conveying the impression that he was more concerned with the recital of his own aspirations. His chance soon came.

'Sounds a dull job,' he said dismissively, so that Jenny, who had said it was a dull job, felt nevertheless an irrational spasm of annoyance. 'Is there nothing doing in Europe?'

'Not that I've seen, and I've been looking. There might be something with the EEC at Brussels or Strasbourg but I don't really fancy the political bit.'

'What about interpreting?'

'You can't make a living at it. There are only about a couple of dozen full-timers in Europe and each of them has two or even three technical specialisations. What will you do? Teach?'

He spotted a taxi and waved it down just beyond Brompton Oratory. He helped Jenny in and ascertained the address, over her formal protestations.

'It's an awful haul away out to Highgate. I'll be perfectly all right.'

'Don't be silly. I'm out at Finchley, it's the right side of town. No, I won't teach.'

This odd directness had surprised her. Later she learned that almost nothing deflected him from his thought path.

'What else can you do?'

'There are a lot of things I *could* do. What I will do is play cricket.'

'Is that a career? Are you good enough.'

'Not quite, and yes.'

'Not quite good enough and it's a career?'

'Not quite a career and yes, I'm good enough. I'd half-a-dozen games in the championship last year and averaged twenty-one. That's not marvellous but it's sufficiently promising for them to have asked me to play for the Seconds next summer and take my chance on being called up.'

'Isn't it a very risky job?'

'Absolutely. It depends on luck, ability and availability

in almost equal measure. That's good. It scores off an awful lot of fellows who could undoubtedly make it.'

'Could you live on it?'

'I've worked it out. You could just about, even as a very run of the mill county player. You could teach during the winter and spring terms.'

'I thought you said you didn't want to teach?'

'I don't.'

He pressed his thigh against hers and she moved away slightly, assuming an interest in the Regent Street lights. He neither followed her nor apologised.

'I've no intention of teaching in a state school, short of actual starvation. No prospects. There never were many, and the falling birthrate's torpedoed things. I'll do it the skipper's way.'

'That's Peter Latimer, that much I do know.'

'Well done, you. Peter has the formula, make your name in the county side, winter at Marlborough, hope for the odd tour that the governors will let you go on.'

'Have you a plan too?'

'Yes. Winter coaching in South Africa. They're desperate to keep the lifelines open to us. They'll take a marginal county player for schools, and if you're any good at all, you'll get a game for one of the provinces.'

'It wouldn't bother you to coach there?'

'Why on earth should it?'

'Apartheid and all that?'

'No.'

His tone was pleasant, and the rest of the journey agreeable. At her house he held on to the taxi and arranged to meet her in the week between Christmas and New Year, and from there matters had developed. They became lovers early in March when she went down to see him at Reading.

They were well-matched in bed and their lovemaking was frequent and enjoyable.

As Jenny became attached to Palfreyman she was exercised by what appeared to be a lack of depth in him. He could turn charm on like a tap, he was intelligent, he was interesting. If thwarted or annoyed, there was no rage, no explosion of verbal or physical fury, rather a murderous silence and, if she had been the offender, total exclusion from his life and thoughts until he came around. The coming around could be a slow process.

Yet they got on pretty well and when he went on the circuit early in May she found that she missed him and shot off at weekends to be with him. He was in the Seconds until the last week in May when an injury let him in at number six, and he held his place until late July when his string of scores in the thirties and forties dried up. He went down to the Seconds again, which explained why he had not been at the Mayor's Reception but at Sidmouth, playing against Devon. Even at that, he'd been called back to the side for the Glamorgan game, but had decided to travel up early on the morning of the match.

Jenny would not hitherto have regarded herself as remotely promiscuous. If she had gone to bed where her mother had not, the practicality of the pill was surely the difference, and it had always been with boys that she really liked after mature deliberation.

Applegarth was not a boy, she did not particularly like him, she did not begin to comprehend her own actions. Apart from the fact that he was married — she'd seen the wife, a pleasant-looking woman — to get involved with a team-mate of Richard shrieked of folly. The chances of keeping such a liaison secret were non-existent.

Had she been drunk that might have been an excuse of a

sort, but although there had been drink at the reception, she had remained quite lucid and rational. Rational! How could she think of her performance as rational? If she had waited to travel down till the Saturday morning, as originally intended, if she had stayed in her room, if Rupert Delaval, seeing her looking lost, had not invited her to join Tilly and himself at the reception . . .

The reception, stuffy but mercifully brief, had ended with the younger element transferring to the God's Wonderful Railway Disco. Applegarth danced not so much with her as at her, he moved very well, with a compact economy which set off the boneless fluidity of Rupert.

It was shameful and unaccountable. For sheer physical attraction, the Antiguan greatly outshone Applegarth. Yet as they danced, and in the DJ's interval when they danced together to records, she felt herself giddy with longing. She was called to the phone for Richard to tell her that he'd be back around nine in the morning, but would possibly go straight to the ground. The DJ was preparing to start the second half of his performance.

'Lover boy, was it?'

'It was Richard, yes. He took a chance I'd be down here already when he couldn't raise me at home.'

'What did he want? Checking up?'

'He's staying at Sidmouth tonight and coming up early tomorrow morning. He's in the side.'

'I know. Steve Elliot's a bloody idiot, breaking a finger at this stage of the season. We need the men.' He put a wounding emphasis on the last word.

'Richard will do his very best.'

'Aye. I'm sure he will.' His words were lost in a cacophony of sound. 'Bugger this for a lark. Let's get out of here.'

For half-an-hour in the bar they sat and talked, Applegarth ascertaining Jenny's room number. He made no attempt to exclude others, indeed invited Steve Elliot over to join them.

'How long'll you be out, Steve?'

'Till next May. The season's over for me.'

'I'm sorry,' Jenny said.

'Lucky for some,' shrugged Elliot good-naturedly enough. 'Young Richard's got the chance to sew it up for us. It's disappointing though. I'm not nearly as philosophical as I sound.'

He went off. Rupert and Tilly went home. By separate, prudent routes Applegarth and Jenny made their way to Room 327. He was, without doubt, the most potent and the most able lover that she had ever had. With his astonishing, understated strength, there was a surprising degree of consideration, physical consideration that was, for he had little in the way of pillow talk. He made no protestations of permanent affection, merely asked her what she would like and made one or two pleasing suggestions.

They made love, rested, then made love again. Jenny was disconcerted when, almost immediately after the second time, he swung his feet to the floor and, unhurriedly, began to dress.

'Where are you going?'

'Home.'

'Isn't it a bit abrupt, even for you?'

He smiled quite warmly at her. 'You don't know if it's abrupt for me. It wouldn't be a good idea for me to stay, would it, in case a certain young would-be cricketer took it into his head to drive through the night?'

'It's not a very clever idea to leave here at — what is it?' — she craned to see her watch on the bedside table — 'three o'clock in the morning. What's the night porter going to think?'

'He's not paid to think along those lines. And any road, I'd be harder put to explain if I was walking out at seven in the morning. Cricketers sometimes keep late hours, y'know, but I should be in my own bed sometime.'

'What about your wife? Should she find out, I mean.'

'I won't tell her, if that's what you're afraid of.'

'Don't you feel at all guilty?'

'No. I may do, some day. Not now. Do you?'

'Very. I'm quite ashamed.' She stood up irresolutely.

'Nonsense. You enjoyed it.'

'I'm even more ashamed of that.' She looked at him almost angrily and said, 'We cannot possibly ever allow this to happen again.'

'That's right, Jenny. And I won't tell Alice, nor should I tell *him*, if I were you.'

They stood for a moment, the girl straight and stiff, the older man looking not unkindly into her vivid blue eyes.

'See it as it was, Jenny. We wanted each other on the night, we were lucky, it worked well. We both know that's all it can be.'

She nodded her head, uncertainly, privately. 'Wham, bam . . .'

He caught her wrists, swept her arms behind her, and kissed her forehead and breasts.

'And thank you, Ma'am. You're a fine girl, with a lovely body. You deserve someone a lot more positive.'

'I think that's hardly for you to say.'

'You're not wrong, and it won't stop me from saying it anyway. Thanks again. It'll make less of a racket if you can close the door behind me.'

At the door, she caught him by the sleeve. 'I can't

promise not to tell Richard, not to own up to him. We've always been very open with each other. It's been that kind of relationship.'

'No one has that kind of relationship. I can't stop you telling him, I can't stop him telling Alice. If I advise you not to, it sounds like I'm protecting my own corner.'

'Aren't you?'

'Yes. And yours, I fancy. Ask yourself before you decide, can you imagine losing him, could you contemplate that?' He turned the handle of the bedroom door. 'Goodnight, Jenny. We were very good. First Eleven class. Unlike some.'

He was already in the corridor, stifling any rejoinder she might have been tempted to make. She closed the door and leaned against it momentarily. The room suddenly felt uncomfortably warm. She went to the window, partially opening the curtains in time to see Applegarth's car swing out of the car park, without lights. As he turned into the seafront road his sidelights came on, then the dipped headlights. The trees, tossing full-leafed in the damp wind, seemed to Jenny to be shaking in incredulous censure of her. She watched the lighthouse flashing out in the bay for a few minutes, reclosed the curtains, and wearily began to run a bath.

CHAPTER 17

The Non-striker

The decision of Richard Palfreyman to run out Applegarth had nothing whatever to do with the brief coupling of the latter and Jenny. He did not then know about it, and of itself it would not perhaps have been motive enough.

He liked Jenny very well — good looking, alluring figure, able to hold her own in conversation. They had a full and pleasant relationship which might conceivably end in marriage at some as yet distant time. It had never inspired in him a maniacal jealousy. You were young, you had no formal attachments, you cut other people out, you would from time to time be cut out yourself. That might well have been his reaction if he had known, but of course he did not.

The animus against Applegarth was much longer-established, and founded on quite different, professional grounds. Or rather, as he was used to think savagely, on the grounds that Applegarth patently did not regard him as being a professional. The Test batsman was certainly not reflecting majority opinion in the County side in this belief. It was typical of Palfreyman that his decision, on hearing of his recall to the side for the Glamorgan match, had been to have a quiet early night at Sidmouth. He was fortunate in having the option, since he was not contracted to bring anyone back in his car. Jenny would not be down at the Brunel till the Saturday morning anyway, and there was no percentage in plunging into the maelstrom of Friday night summer traffic in the West Country. If he left at six in the morning things would be much calmer, driving much more relaxed.

He sat in the residents' lounge and, an uninterested eye on the Nine O'Clock News, took stock. At this stage of the season there could be no further chances. His task was to hold his place until mid-September, knowing that until now, he had not done quite enough to be sure that the County's interest in him would be renewed the following year.

Pluses and minuses. Swings and roundabouts. Strengths and deficiencies. He tried to submit himself to a rigorous, objective assessment, neither exaggerating his assets nor overemphasising his weaknesses.

He was the five feet ten inches that he had been at sixteen, a height for which he would have settled very happily two years earlier when he just topped five feet. In the course of a spectacular summer he lengthened remarkably, until he was sure that he would comfortably pass the six foot mark. This did not happen, in the autumn it all stopped as suddenly as it had begun, to his considerable disappointment. No bad thing perhaps in the end, he was tall enough for few desirable girls to embarrass him, and the highest places in cricket did not offer themselves only to giants, whereas in basketball, say, his height would have been an absolute bar to a professional career.

The News finished and he paid close attention to the

weather forecast. It was good, and so therefore should the crowd be at Westercote tomorrow. He quickened a little with the thought. When the ring was well-filled, there was the desire to do particularly well, the little strut in one's stride in the field, a worked-at nonchalance in the conversational exchanges with the crowd on the boundary rope. He lacked the marvellous rapport which such as Jack Simmons of Lancashire had, even with opposing crowds, and he was not loved as Rupert Delaval, or admired, like Applegarth, but he was building his own little claque of supporters.

Fielding did not come specially easy to him. He had the large feet and stiff gait of the non-natural, and the fact that he wore spectacles in the field gave him an owlish, donnish look and conveyed the impression, on the very few occasions when he failed to pick up the flight of the ball, that he had been dozing. What he did have were marvellous, bucket-sized hands, so that any lofted shot to the deep that could be run down was a chance accepted. As an outfield catcher, he was in the class of Alan Ealham of Kent, invaluable for disposing of tail-enders who had a mind to swing the bat. His bowling was erratic, but sufficiently promising to suggest that, given the long spells needed by all young spinners, it might well blossom.

It would require to be a hardy plant that could flourish in the face of Applegarth's cold, blighting and continuous scorn. Palfreyman initially had borne no resentment for this, it was part of the mystique of county cricket that newcomers were given a hard time of it by grizzled old pros. What increasingly angered him was what appeared to be the England player's perverse determination never to accord him credit under any circumstances. If he pulled off a particularly good catch, any words of commendation which Applegarth had went to the bowler, no matter that the ball might have been an appalling long-hop redeemed by a blindingly brilliant catch. If he played a gritty little innings of thirty or so, Frank would say audibly to Masterton that one of the differences between the dabbler and the true professional was that in similar circumstances the pro would go on to get seventy or eighty. Or worse, he would make a barbed remark to the effect that one of the nicest things about club cricketers, as opposed to the county variety, was that they were much less selfish — they were always prepared to get out and give their colleagues a knock.

Palfreyman was not lacking in courage and he had, earlier in the season, tackled Applegarth on his hostile, uninterested attitude towards him. It had been a revealing rather than a productive conversation.

'I honestly don't mind being slagged for my mistakes, Frank, and I'll make a lot, I'm a young player. But I'd make fewer if I got the odd word of encouragement when I do something good.'

'Do something good then, and we'll see.'

'What about yesterday's catch at long leg then?'

'That's what you were put there for. Everybody knows Botham will hook anything, given half a chance. Skipper told Steve to ping one in, Both hooked it, badly, you caught it. Skipper thought it out, not that it required a great deal in the way of thinking.'

'Was it part of his plan that I'd run twenty yards and catch it at full stretch?'

'If you'd been squarer, as you should have been, you could have caught it in your mouth.'

Richard Palfreyman looked narrowly at him. 'Is it just me, Frank? I notice you encourage one or two of the other younger players. And not just the younger players. Maybe I should burnt-cork my face and practice an Antiguan accent?'

Applegarth's face was expressionless. 'You can't paint ability on that easily. You're right, I don't particularly like you. I very much doubt if you'll be good enough in the long run, and you're not serious about the job.'

'How do you mean, not serious? I never miss a net, I never skip circuit training, unlike your pal Bernie, the valiant stumper. Come on, senior man, be consistent, don't tell me you find *his* attitude particularly professional?'

'Maybe aye, maybe no. But he's only got one thing on his mind, he's not trying to have the best of both worlds. I watched you at Northampton the other day. You spent every lunch and tea interval with their University people, Boyd-Moss, Peck, and what's-his-name?'

'Mills,' Palfreyman provided sullenly. The observation had angered him in its accuracy. 'What about our skipper then? He's in the same position as me.'

'No, he's not. He's a slightly better player.' He hit the adverb heavily.

'He'd be interested to hear you say that.'

'He's heard me, many times. He's never made a hundred against another county, he's never taken five wickets in an innings. If he forgot about the teaching he might be pretty useful. Nothing more.'

Palfreyman was angry, but even more, curious. 'You're very set against what you might call the University cricketer, aren't you?'

The other man nodded grimly. 'I've cause to be. I came through in the old Gents and Players time. In my second season I was left out for the month of August, having just hit three consecutive fifties, to accommodate C.T.S.

Pendle, Repton and Cambridge. Qualification, father had been great buddy of our then President. In fairness, the lad had a stylish cover drive if anyone was obliging enough to pitch it on the half-volley outside the off-stump. People like Brian Statham and Alan Moss would hardly bowl that kind of ball once in an innings. Know what this lot did? We took him on as secretary so that he could stay as captain for the next season. He made 310 runs in 41 innings. You could look it up, *Wisden 1964*. I could have been here half a century and they'd never have offered me the bloody secretary's job, although I could have made just as spectacular a balls-up of the correspondence as he did.'

So that was it, Richard thought, the old social bit, envy and insecurity arising from the senior professional's background. Fair enough too, to a certain extent, it must have been galling to be sent down to the Seconds to make way for an untalented sprig. For a moment he felt almost sympathetic towards Applegarth.

The last vestiges of that sympathy were ground out ruthlessly in the first innings of the match against Glamorgan at Westercote which marked his return to the County's First Eleven. Palfreyman, having played and missed a couple of times early on, stayed to defend resolutely and, eventually, to bat with fluency. When he was finally caught in the gully off a savage cut, his score stood at 77, comfortably his highest in first-class cricket, and top score for his side. He and Applegarth added more than 60 for the seventh wicket, during which time he scored run for run with his more illustrious partner. Apart from one wrenched, grudging 'Shot!' for a particularly fine leg glance the neat, compact Applegarth confined himself to 'Yes!', 'No!', 'Wait!', 'Look for two!'

On the fall of his own wicket — he was last out — Palfreyman had left the crease, trying to keep the elation from his face as he moved with modestly-uplifted bat through the rows of members who applauded him vigorously. He would have forgiven Applegarth all for a 'Well done, son!' or 'A few more like that and you'll make it.' Applegarth, however, was not in the dressing-room, and neither when the teams took the field for Glamorgan's second innings, nor at any subsequent time did he make any reference to Palfreyman's singular triumph.

It was at that moment that Palfreyman conceived the desire and the purpose of damaging his team-mate, although he was as yet uncertain how he might do this. Through Alice? The thought came quickly and was discarded even more quickly. She was at least ten years older, seemed undetachable, and there were those two noisy brats. More important, success, which in any event was unlikely and unwanted (Alice's wholesome freshness made little appeal), would inevitably mean his parting from the County.

His plan shaped itself with luminous clarity in the course of their own second innings. He knew how dear the toppling of the batting record was to his censorious colleague's heart, knew also that Applegarth was batting with such assurance and conviction that the odds were overwhelmingly in favour of that record being smashed. The fact that the player about to be removed from the record-books had the name of Oswald Julian Trefusis Manderley, and a corresponding background, would add savour, piquancy perhaps, to the achievement.

There was no guarantee that Applegarth still might not get his ninth ton, but time was running out. So too was the weather. The forecast for the next few days was bad, and while Worcester, venue for the last match of all, was certainly a batsman's track, the home side were quite capable of batting the whole of the first day, should they win the toss, and, even on the best of wickets, strange things often happened when a side set out in pursuit of a mammoth total.

The beauty of it all was that the game could easily be won without Applegarth. Eighty odd to get and any God's amount of batting to come. He himself was in confident mood, having gone quickly to fifteen and with his first innings knock immediately recognised by promotion to number five, a modification to the batting order that had initially raised a few eyebrows in the pavilion but seemed to have been inspired.

He had banked that instinct and years of training would take over Applegarth on the crucial ball. It had to be such an obvious single from the other end that Frank would arrive at the non-striker's end automatically. Glamorgan had just taken short-leg away to reinforce the slips; even at that it still seemed to him, Palfreyman, a cautiously-set field.

He saw Applegarth come down the wicket and keep coming past his point of no return. He saw the incredulous, startled look on the Humberside man's face as his own lips moved almost inaudibly. He saw the bails at the other end go up, and finally he saw Applegarth's retreating back.

Palfreyman's look of appalled contrition was sufficiently convincing to wring a couple of 'Hard luck, son's' from the Welshmen, though his heart skipped a little as umpire Ken Carpenter gave him a considering, lingering look. He put it out of his mind as he got on with the business of winning the game which would make the County all but impossible to catch in the Championship. Whatever stick he had to take for the run-out would be administered lightly in the hour of victory with the pennant all but there for the breaking out, and Applegarth in theory still with a chance of that individual record which should in any event rightly yield precedence to the collective success.

Then, with the speed of a snick through slips, the innings had disintegrated and it had all gone irretrievably wrong. Three quick wickets fell at the other end while he collected another ten runs. He played Malcolm Nash pleasantly back down the wicket for a two. The next ball moved back off the seam and he got a very faint inside edge to thigh to the gloves of Eifion Jones standing up. The keeper hurled the ball in the air with a pardonably gleeful roar — it was a fine catch.

He was glad that he had walked, even if the first two steps away from the wicket had been involuntary. He walked with downcast eyes and trailing bat towards a pavilion that seemed to get no nearer, no matter how often he put one foot after the other. The few expressions of condolence that he could identify sounded perfunctory and totally lacking in conviction. He, in his pride, in his arrogance, in his animosity towards another player, had dashed the hopes of hundreds here today, and there would be an accounting.

He remembered going into the dressing-room where only Applegarth was, although it was his impression that there may have been someone through in the shower. He could find no conventional stammering of apology in the face of the other's furious glare. He turned to lay his bat and gloves on the bench, and then he was spun round from behind and struck, with a fist and perhaps the edge of a bat. It was difficult to be quite certain; he was dazed and had bled quite a bit. He could recall trying to roll away from the attack while on the ground.

Dr Winant had been very good about taking him to the hospital and seeing that the treatment he received was prompt and thorough. The doctor was scrupulous in saying nothing of Applegarth's involvement. It was unlikely that he would have criticised Richard for his gross error, but neither did he offer false comfort.

When Palfreyman got back to the hotel, head aching slightly, face stiff and bruised, he had a brief word with Sir Anthony. The President informed him that he and Applegarth would be asked to appear before a sub-committee the following morning.

'If it's up to me, Sir Anthony, I'd much rather let things drop. When I think of the stupidity of the run-out, of what it cost the County, of how it snatched the record from Frank, I'm just sick. I can perfectly imagine how he must have felt.'

Sir Anthony looked at him puzzledly. 'That's to your credit, of course, my dear fellow. It cannot, however, be "up to you" as you put it. It was hardly a normal reaction, was it?'

'I don't know, sir. I've never been run out by an idiot on my own side when within sight of my ninth century of the season.' His attempt at a boyish smile was transformed to a wincing grimace of the swollen face.

'I doubt if you'd resort to assault and battery if it happened. You'd be quite entitled to press charges against Applegarth, y'know.'

'There's no question of that, Sir Anthony.'

'That's magnanimous of you, must say I'm relieved to hear you say it. Wouldn't do the club any good. You know how the Press distort things when they get hold of a notion. By the way, don't talk to them, they're scarcely to be trusted, even the best of them.'

'I'll say nothing, Sir Anthony. I don't cut a very heroic

figure in this episode anyway. I hope nothing'll happen to Frank.'

'He'll get a full and fair hearing. You'll certainly be able to clear up a few points for us.'

'I'll do my best.'

'Off you go then. I'd get an early night. But of course, your girl's here, isn't she?'

'Jenny'll understand, sir.'

'I'm sure she will,' the President said with no very marked conviction. 'Nine-thirty sharp at the ground then, in fact if everyone's there, we might be able to start a few minutes before that. Half-an-hour or an hour should do it. On you go then. Remember me to your lady.'

'I'll do that, Sir Anthony.'

CHAPTER 18

The Hearing: 1

Sir Anthony was fairly sure of one thing as he settled into the tiny committee room of the Crippledyke ground at exactly nine-fifteen on the Wednesday morning. They could take as much time over the inquiry as they liked for the day was grey and remorselessly dripping. The heavy cloud was down to the spires of the motionless trees, there was not a break in sight. The gate-men had turned up out of duty, but they had only to deal with the very occasional lunatic optimist. Perhaps the weather might change with the turn of the tide, but that thought required a massive investment in hope. Certainly the Warwickshire lads were not breaking their necks to get down to the ground. There was a funereal inactivity in the normally clattering refreshment tents where the setting up would have been going on, and out in the middle Tom Killock and his assistant stood uncertainly immobile. No one hurried to Crippledyke from the Grove Café.

The President had rather surprised Peter Latimer and the chairman of the cricket committee, Ken Lightbody, with his brisk effectiveness: in small details, note-pads and glasses of water were on the rickety trestle table; more tell-ingly, a policeman was stationed at the pavilion door and another outside the window of the committee room. Sir Anthony was determined that the statement which the Press would eventually carry would be that agreed upon by this sub-committee.

He looked along at his two colleagues and cleared his throat with a peremptory, irritated noise.

'I would propose, gentlemen, briefly to recapitulate the events of yesterday afternoon. Frank Applegarth, on being run out by young Palfreyman, attacked him in the dressing room, causing bruising to his face and a gash in his cheek which required three stitches. He might well have inflicted more damage had he not mercifully been restrained by Bernie Masterton, yourself, Peter, and Harry Adams. I believe those are the salient facts?'

The others assented.

'I would further take it that we would agree that this was a distressing, indeed, unsavoury, episode which should clearly be dealt with by just such a sub-committee as this?'

Again the heads nodded.

'Who did you think we should see, Sir Anthony?' Ken Lightbody asked, pushing a Biro pen through his grey, wavy hair. 'The two people concerned, obviously, the other two who dragged them apart, and yourself, Peter, of course.'

'I thought we might have a word with the umpires, infor-mally at least.'

'They won't have reported the incident to Lord's, Presi-dent.'

'Indeed, Peter. There was no reason for them to do so. It was just an ordinary run-out as far as they were concerned, but they might have seen something or heard something.

We'd simply ask for their help, I thought.'

'Should Frank have somebody from the Professional Cricketers' Association to advise him?'

'You mean on the lines of the soldier's friend, Ken?'

'That's it.'

'Maybe eventually. Depends where we see that our findings are taking us.' Stork-like and stiff, he stood up. 'I'll fetch Applegarth in. I must say it's not the way I'd looked to spend this morning twenty-four hours ago. Reminds me of defaulters' parade.'

Applegarth had obviously been waiting at hand for he was in the room a few seconds later, giving his usual impression of taut economy of movement, his thinning fair hair like a Noel Coward toupee, his dress an odd mixture of blazer, cricket shirt and checked sports slacks. He was invited to sit himself down, and Sir Anthony then read to him the agreed facts of the case, stopping from time to time to obtain the confirmation of the other two. After a dozen sentences or so, he stopped.

'This is very awkward,' he said, almost angrily. 'There's no use disguising it's a disciplinary situation, we are here representing the County as employers. I'd still prefer to keep it as informal as I can, so Frank and Sir Anthony, rather than Mr Applegarth and President, would be my choice.'

'Fine,' Applegarth nodded curtly.

'Do you disagree with the facts as I've read them over to you?'

'No.'

'Then can you explain the violence of your actions against a team-mate?' Sir Anthony leaned forward. 'Believe me, we're not unsympathetic. No-one has wanted the Championship more fervently than I, no-one has seen more

170

bad sides here over the years . . . and we know how set you were on topping Ossie Manderley's record. But we cannot be expected to condone a situation in which as a result of your lashing out, another of our players ends up in hospital. I can say in all literal truth I was shocked.'

Applegarth's head had nodded at various points in the President's exposition.

'You said, Sir Anthony, you found my actions shocking. I think that's literally true, they were performed in a state of shock, or maybe fury.'

'There can't be any room in cricket for such a violent reaction to an honest mistake.'

'Exactly. I'm in my twenty-first season as a professional cricketer and I've never reacted violently to an *honest* mistake.'

It was Peter Latimer who first picked up on the emphasis.

'What are you driving at, Frank? What are you suggesting?'

Applegarth looked at them, unwavering before their gaze. 'I'm stating, not suggesting, that the run-out was no mistake, that it was a deliberate action on the part of Palfreyman.'

Sir Anthony's incredulous 'I say!' was smothered by Latimer's 'Come off it, Frank!' and Lightbody's 'Why in God's name would he want to do that?'

'Look,' Sir Anthony said patiently, as to a dim, froward child, 'it was a dreadful run-out. The blame was totally young Palfreyman's, nobody's going to argue about that. It was a monumental piece of stupidity and cost us the game, without doubt. But that's a vastly different thing from saying that he ran you out with malice aforethought.'

Lightbody looked at Applegarth with no very friendly

171

eye. 'I'll repeat my question, Frank. Why in God's name would he want to do that?'

'To get at me. To prevent my going for the record.' He spread out his hands. 'I had it, there for the taking.'

The President nodded. 'If ever a century looked certain, it was yesterday. Let me understand you, Frank, are you saying that young Palfreyman deliberately threw the game?'

'I'm not saying that,' with a dogged head-shake. 'With just eighty odd to get and more than half the side still there to get them, it seems quite likely to me that he thought it could easily be done without my help. The two things are separate, gentlemen. I repeat, he wanted to get at me, not necessarily at the County.'

Lightbody returned to the attack, twisting his stocky body in his chair.

'He's still got to have a reason, even if we accepted such a fantastic notion.'

'Not too hard to find, maybe. We don't get on. He thinks I give him a hard time of it.'

'Does he?' Sir Anthony's question was addressed to Peter Latimer.

'No more, I'd have thought, than he gives all newcomers to the side. No more, I'd have thought, than he gave me when I was a colt.'

'Hang on a minute, Peter,' Ken Lightbody interjected. 'I don't recall his having given Rupert a hard time. Rupert is loud in your praises, Frank.'

'He was far from home,' said Applegarth defensively, 'and a great trier. And I think he'd tell you he's had the rough side of my tongue when he's bowled like a fool, or spilled a catch.'

Sir Anthony dragged the meeting back to the crucial

172

point, intent.

'How can you be sure that the run-out was deliberate?'

'You all saw the incident?'

Three nods.

'Did it seem a safe run to you, gentlemen?'

Three more, with the captain chipping in.

'We needn't waste time debating the merits of the run. The run was there, it was a good call, I expect Palfreyman will tell us that again when we see him. He simply failed to respond. Damn it, Frank, we've all slept on safe singles in our time.'

'And shouted "No!" when we have done,' the veteran gritted. 'Or even "No, sorry!" I'll ask *you* a question. Did you hear Palfreyman say anything like that?'

The three conferred and, after deliberation, stated that it was their firm recollection that Palfreyman had said nothing at all.

'You're wrong there, he very definitely said something to me when I got up that end.'

'What did he say?'

'I'll tell you what he said, Sir Anthony. He said, quite softly and very definitely, "Good-bye".'

'Really, Applegarth,' — the President momentarily forgot his self-defined protocol — 'we're in the realms of fantasy now.'

'I was as close to him as I am to you now, President,' said Applegarth with an immediately equivalent formality.

'Anybody else hear it?' Lightbody wanted to know.

'I don't know. That doesn't affect the fact that he said it. We were practically eyeball to eyeball. I know what I know, and one of the things I know is that I won't ever play again on the same side as that despicable, cheating young bastard.'

'I would advise you, Frank,' the President said, with generous inconsistency of title, 'not to make any statement of that sort until we have determined the outcome of this hearing. Is that all, gentlemen? Anything else we can usefully ask at this stage? Right. Will you arrange, Frank, to stay on the ground please? We'll be looking to need you again in another hour or so. Remember that you are forbidden to discuss any part of these proceedings with the Press.'

Peter Latimer saw his colleague to the pavilion door, partly as a genuine courtesy, partly to keep him out of the path of Palfreyman whom he knew was waiting in his car outside.

Palfreyman's evidence was in essence that which he had previously given to Sir Anthony. He made even less of an attempt this time to justify his lack of response to Applegarth's call.

'It was an appalling piece of cricket. What else can I say? I was physically and mentally on my heels. We'd just hared a three, only a two really, but Frank had turned it into a three, he really motored. As the bowler ran up I remember thinking, "I'm pretty puffed, I hope the old lad just blocks this one."'

'It was the easiest of runs, Richard,' his captain said reprovingly. 'You could have taken it at a walk.'

'I simply froze, and that's the truth. I hadn't even the wit to notice that apparently Malcolm Nash had pushed Llewellyn deeper at mid-off.'

'For Heaven's sake, why didn't you call? That way we'd have lost the run but kept the wicket.'

'I tried to, but the words wouldn't come out. Sheer panic, I suppose. I think I did croak "Go back" but it was far too late by then.'

'That's not what Frank says you called,' said Sir

Anthony, his expression uneasy, his voice troubled.

'What's his version? May I know?' Palfreyman looked nervously around him.

'I'm sorry to have to say this, but I must. He told us that your words to him were "Good-bye".'

'That's outrageous! It's a damned, wicked lie! He's saying I ran him out on purpose!'

'Yes, Richard. That's what he's saying.'

'Do you believe me capable of that? And here's me having spent all last night feeling so desperately sorry for him.' The weals stood out on his tautened face. 'I admired that man, I admired him in the way an autograph hunter would. He's all the batsmen I'd ever dream of being. And he could say that about me? Has anyone else said they heard me say that, or something like it?'

'We haven't asked anyone else yet. We will. Don't distress yourself, Richard, we'll investigate very fully.'

'His judgment's been affected by the disappointment.' Palfreyman's voice was low, as if he were explaining Applegarth's actions for his own satisfaction rather than for that of anyone else. 'I'm worse off than he is. He'll always be the chap who so nearly won us the Championship, I'll be the buffoon who chucked it away. Like those poor sods who miss a last-minute penalty at Wembley and have to watch themselves missing it for the rest of their lives.'

'At least you're spared the action replays, Richard,' Lightbody said in a lightly frost-tinged voice. He had found the apologia unaffecting, although far from subscribing to Applegarth's version.

After Palfreyman had departed to the same injunctions on availability and silence that had been administered to the striker, the three men conferred briefly. They had discounted the notion of involving any Glamorgan players. These had packed up and gone on to the next game anyway and, at least at this stage, there was a wish to keep the matter totally within the home dressing-room if at all possible. Since, however, the two umpires, Dodd and Carpenter, were staying on for the Warwickshire game, it seemed only sensible to see if they had any light to shed. Certainly brief passages with Masterton and Harry Adams had not been too illuminating.

The umpires came in together from an early look at the wicket with the dismal news that there would be no chance of play before lunch, and prospects thereafter would depend on an almost immediate cessation of the rain. Both men added their voices to the universal belief that the run was very much there and that Frank had been abundantly justified in going for it.

'Did either of you hear a call?'

'Not at all, not in the sense of a call,' Carpenter explained. 'Frank simply played the checked drive and sauntered off down the wicket. It was such a blindingly obvious run that he probably didn't feel the need.'

'Did Palfreyman say anything?'

'I didn't hear a thing from square leg,' Charles Dodd said.

'Mr Carpenter?'

'I thought I heard him say something in a low voice. But you'll understand I was on the move, looking for a run-out.' He grinned at their astonishment. 'I thought they might just try to turn the one into a two. That's how safe a run I thought it was.'

'What did you think you heard Palfreyman say?'

Carpenter took the plunge. 'It sounded a little like "Good-bye".'

The three men looked at each other. For a moment only the rain on the windows broke the silence.

Sir Anthony looked at Carpenter sternly.

'You would be moving quickly to get into position?'

'Of course.'

'So you could not be quite sure?'

'I could not be sure at all. I was careful to say that I thought I heard him say that.'

'But it could well have been something similar?'

'Yes, I imagine so.'

'Something like "Go back!" for example?'

'That would appear a more natural thing to say. A still more natural thing to shout.'

'Mr Carpenter, Mr Dodd, you well appreciate that this situation does not redound to the County's advantage and is not of our choosing. We may have to take some form of disciplinary action, and if we have to, we want to make sure we've taken the best evidence and information available to us. We're grateful for your help. Mr Carpenter, could you state definitely that Richard Palfreyman used the form of words you thought you heard?'

'Do you mean in a formal, legal situation?'

'If it came to that, yes.'

'No.' And on being pressed he became balky and somewhat huffy. There was nothing to be done but to thank the two umpires for their assistance.

'You'll be able to catch up on the reading today, I'm afraid, Mr Dodd.'

''Fraid so, Sir Anthony. I'll take this young feller' — indicating his colleague — 'out to have another look about twelve. It won't do the slightest good, but it will let the members see that we're trying, and that always goes down well.'

The two men, shrugging anoraks back on over cricket sweaters, went off.

Sir Anthony stared at the table, twirling a pencil through his fingers like a drum-majorette's baton. At last he spoke.

'I don't like the imputation of malice that's coming through here. Fortunately, I don't believe it. I daren't believe it, for the game isn't playable on any basis but trust. Peter?'

'I think the old boy's gone a bit over the top on this one, Sir Anthony. We all know how intense Frank can be.'

'What about the bad blood between them?'

'It's there. Maybe I should, as skipper, have knocked heads together. But it's Frank's way. He's never going to make it easy for anyone who can't meet his perfectionist standards.'

'What do you think, Ken?'

Lightbody, having imprinted the ceiling on his mind, put his chair back on four scraping legs and fixed the other two.

'I agree with you, Chairman, that malice would make this game unplayable. We certainly can't, in this instance, establish it to courtroom standards of proof, and increasingly these days, that's what we'd have to do. But malice is a human vice, it happens in other spheres of human activity, we'd be foolish to imagine that cricket has some heaven-sent dispensation from it.'

Sir Anthony snorted. 'You don't have to love your team-mates to play well with them. Half the great batting partnerships of history couldn't stand the sight of each other after stumps. Maybe we've been spoiled here in the County, when you think of the kind of squabbling that's been going on in the Yorkshire dressing-room since Ronnie Burnett's time.'

Peter Latimer grinned. 'C'mon, Sir Anthony, I'm no

great admirer of the Tykes but you'd admit that very few of their disagreements have been as spectacular, or as public, as this one.'

'You may be right. More to the point, what should our decision be here?'

Lightbody ticked off his fingers. 'It should be salutary but not savage — it should be something which we're pretty sure the generality of members will go for — it should be seen to be equitable.'

'Then, let's take Applegarth, he's the cause of our being here.'

'Common assault,' Lightbody said, 'he'd have been nicked for it outside.'

'I take it a fine would be appropriate. What should it be? It has to be significant. I would suggest five hundred pounds,' said Sir Anthony magisterially.

'Too much,' the other two said in unison.

'It's got to hurt,' Sir Anthony said frowning. 'All right, then, how about four hundred pounds?'

'Three hundred and fifty would be better,' Latimer began, but Ken Lightbody sided with the President and so the figure was determined.

'And, of course, a warning as to future conduct, and a public apology to young Palfreyman.' The President looked at the two dubious faces with unconcealed irritation. 'Damn it, the lad's been thumped and publicly humiliated. The members will expect an apology, otherwise it looks as if we're saying that Applegarth was in some way justified in the action he took. Do we need to vote on it?'

Latimer had the momentary thought that the old man must have been fairly formidable in his Army days.

'No? Good. Let's fetch Frank Applegarth back in.'

Applegarth listened in silence as the President impressed

upon him the gravity of his offence. Sir Anthony pointed out that since there was a fine involved, he might wish to take legal advice, and he was of course free to do so.

'That's all right, Sir Anthony. I hit him in a public place, I don't deny hitting him. I'll cheerfully pay the money.'

In this reply the desired note of reconciliation did not appear prominently. The sub-committee's misgivings were compounded by his next sentence.

'However, gentlemen, I must tell you that I will not be apologising to Palfreyman now or at any time. Further, I have to tell you that I cannot play for any side for which he may have been selected.'

There was no piece of paper in his hands but it sounded like a prepared and rehearsed speech. Peter Latimer did his best to bail out his star batsman.

'I don't think this is the time or place to make statements like that, Frank.'

'Sorry, skipper, it's the way I feel. I won't play with that slimy bastard again. Anywhere, anytime.'

'What you are asking for,' Sir Anthony said icily, 'is for power of veto over team selection. That's an immoderate demand.'

'I'm simply saying we can't be in the same side. I'm not suggesting you can't pick him.'

Sir Anthony and his colleagues went into a huddle while Applegarth was asked to wait outside briefly. When he returned the wish to do well by him was manifest in the President's face.

'We are asking you to say or do nothing for twenty-four hours. Today's play will be washed out officially in an hour or so. Go home and talk it over with your wife. You owe her that. And maybe you owe the County that much too, Frank. It's been a long, and I'd like to think, a happy association. We will make no statement until tomorrow; if we tell the Press we've still got some evidence to consider, that should hold them. I can promise you that we will say nothing to them.'

'It makes sense, Frank,' Ken Lightbody said.

'I'll certainly talk it over with Alice tonight,' Applegarth said slowly. 'She's entitled to know what's happening. But at the end of the day, it'll make no difference to my decision.'

'It may have to, Frank,' the President snapped, 'it may well have to.'

CHAPTER 19

The Hearing: 2

'That's your last word, Frank?'

Alice Applegarth sat on the floor of their lounge, legs tucked underneath her, looking rather young to be the mother of two roistering lads.

'You're quite sure this is what you're going to do?'

'Quite sure,' Applegarth said, quietly.

Outside, Locking Hill was the identical rainswept misery of the previous evening.

'It seems to be our week for heart to hearts,' — Alice managed an uneasy smile. 'It's a fairly hefty fine, love, I must say.'

'The fine's the least of it. I thought it might even be more.'

'Tell me again what they want from you. The fine and a public apology to young Richard?'

'An apology to young Richard, university graduate, slimy bastard and cheat.'

'And you don't feel you can do that, Frank?'

'No. We've been married long enough for you to realise what a daft question that was.'

'Would it be such a terrible thing to say sorry?' Alice per-

182

sisted. 'He did get a pretty red face in front of the members and his girl, after all.'

'It'd have been a bloody sight redder if Bernie and the skipper hadn't pulled me off him when they did. There's not really any point in discussing it, Alice, I told the committee I wouldn't play in the same side as him ever again.'

'Will they wear that?'

'I doubt it. Hired hand dictating to the top brass and all that sort of thing. Sir Anthony virtually said as much.'

'You'd think after all you've done for the County . . .'

'A very dangerous line of thought, Alice. At the end of the day all horses and old pros get put out to grass. They're probably telling each other back at the hotel right now, "The game has to be greater than even the most talented individual, old boy".'

Alice readjusted the folds of her washed-blue dirndl skirt, shaking her head in tiny movements of incomprehension. 'But you said last night you thought you'd get a fair hearing.'

'You said that, last night,' her husband reminded her. 'And you were quite right, the committee were very fair, they're desperate to see the matter patched up amicably and everyone back at the work bench. It's just that they don't believe me, Sir Anthony especially.'

'You've always been straight in your dealings with them.'

Applegarth, face graven, wondered about the inflection of the last word, and decided he was looking for non-existent nuances. He was yet sufficiently discomposed that his words came rather faster than usual.

'It's not that he thinks I'm a liar. It's simply that he cannot conceive of any cricketer doing something like that. In his book, a cricketer is a man of honour, therefore incapable of such an act.'

Alice stared into the fire which was unseasonably welcome, unseasonably bright.

'You couldn't have misheard?'

'No way.'

'It's really got to you, hasn't it? You find it just as difficult to believe as Sir Anthony.' He nodded. 'I don't blame them for not believing it. I'd be very slow to credit it of somebody if I hadn't witnessed it.'

'I've only one other question,' Alice said with the dogged affection of a pet approaching a master of uncertain temper. 'Have you ever known of anything like this before?'

Applegarth's eyes looked beyond her, for a moment he said nothing. Then: 'Nothing like this. You get times when a night watchman's there too long in the morning and you want a recognised bat in. Maybe on a Sunday, somebody's having a sticky time in a JPL knock. Captain'll say, half fun, whole earnest, on the fall of a wicket, "In you go, Frank, and run that bugger out!" But you'd pass on the message, give him the chance to liven up.' His face was set in a kind of anger at the way his approach to the game was being extracted from him. 'You have to play cricket dead straight. It's quite easy to cheat. Quite a lot of the time you'd get away with it. If I were a baker, or a policeman, I'd want to be a straight one. I happen to be a cricketer.' He took an impatient turn around the room. 'I don't want to say any more on that area, I sound like a bloody Hallelujah.'

It was time for Alice to express a major concern. 'If it goes a certain way, Frank, this could be the end of you with County?'

'Little doubt of that, lass.'

'What about your Testimonial? All our future plans are based on it.'

'It would go, of course.'

'Of course. Twenty thousand pounds perhaps! Just like that! For that money I might be thinking of an apology.'

'You might. But I don't think so. I can't see you apologising to someone that you knew had done you great damage, not by inexperience or even honest-to-God pardonable stupidity, but quite deliberately, and had actually enjoyed doing it.'

The phone rang. He reached down and placed his hands heavily on her shoulders, making it impossible for her to rise to answer it.

'Let it ring.'

'It's possibly important, Frank.'

'For the caller, maybe, not for us. I said I'd talk to nobody tonight and I meant it.' The ringing lasted for two minutes then, discouraged, ceased.

'Good,' said Applegarth, indulging in a half-smile. 'only five minutes to the Ten O'Clock Sports News anyway. We don't want anyone rabbiting on through that.'

'Might you get another County?'

He nodded with strong conviction. 'I'd be astonished if I didn't.'

'Who's looking?'

'Derbyshire. The Notts batting isn't that hot. Wrong end of the country, of course, but it's only a seller's market to a limited extent.'

'Yorkshire don't seem able to make two hundred and fifty this season to save themselves.'

'When did they change the qualification rule? Did I miss it on the mid-day News?'

'Frank, how stupid of me. I'm sorry.'

'That's all right. Story of my life.' He grew more serious. 'You realise, Alice, that at my stage, the very best I could

185

hope for would be a two-year contract. Maybe, with a lot of luck, a single season after that. We could put any thought of a testimonial firmly out of our heads. There's no way that I could be with another county long enough now to qualify.' He grimaced as a thought struck him. 'In fact, if our lot wanted to be really sticky about it, they could tie up my registration so that I missed the first part of next season. But I think they'd let me go if I went quietly.'

'We could make out.' Alice's voice had genuine confidence.

'I'd be away almost all summer, probably. It'd be strange coming home for away games.' He looked at the mantel clock and, swearing, turned on the radio in the nick of time.

'. . . At Lord's, where they were luckier with the weather than elsewhere, it was possible to make a start just after half-past four. Mike Brearley won the toss, inserted Northants, and by close of play the visitors had slumped to sixty seven for five. Four of the wickets, Willey, Larkins, Cooke and nightwatchman Sharp, fell to the lethal pace of Wayne Daniel . . .'

Applegarth depressed the button.

'Don't you want the other scores?'

'They were only playing at Folkestone apart from that. What a bloody captain Brearley is!' The tone made it clear that this was a profound compliment. 'Loses almost a day, sticks them in, he's already two bonus points up, heading for four. Northants won't make 150 now.'

'Why wouldn't he bat?'

'How many runs for one bonus point?'

'One hundred and fifty, I think.'

'Check. How long to make that?'

'Two hours, the way you lot potter about in county matches, maybe more.'

'I'm proud of you. Now, how many wickets for a bowling point?'

'Three.'

'How quickly could you take three wickets?'

'In three balls, I suppose.'

'There's your answer. Percentages. You could bowl a side out in the time it'd take you to make a hundred. Best skipper in the Championship by a mile.'

'University man, isn't he?' said his wife, greatly daring, and was rewarded by that relatively rare event, an Applegarth grin.

Over supper she said, 'They might withdraw the requirement to apologise.'

'Wouldn't help, would it?'

'I suppose not. So really the only hope is that Richard Palfreyman will decide to move on.'

'I don't see that. There'd be no great demand for his services anywhere else. He's not good enough at this level.'

'I've often heard you say that very unlikely people have made it on the county circuit.'

'Not as unlikely as he is.' An overhead noise drew him up. 'Boys! Do you want the hammering of your lives with the flat of my bat?'

On that rhetorical question he went upstairs and effectively closed the conversation. Alice went on clearing the supper things mechanically. In the midst of the bridesmaids, the Rolls Royce, the reception, the long-unseen relatives, there had been a sentence about better or worse. The comfortable financial props had been knocked from under them. Frank was dour, undemonstrative, maddeningly matter-of-fact. She was luckier than the girl Jenny, for all that. Her man was not a cheat.

* * * * * *

187

The three men, Sir Anthony, Ken Lightbody and Peter Latimer, looked at each other ruefully in the little room which Frank Applegarth had just left. He had, once more, politely, without heat but very definitely, declined either to apologise to Richard Palfreyman, or to make himself available for selection in any side of which the latter was a member.

Repeated expostulations and entreaties had failed to shift him, and eventually he had been asked to withdraw to allow the committee time to reconsider their course of action.

'I can't believe it,' Sir Anthony spluttered, 'when you think of how much is at stake for the fellow.' He shook his head despondently, and looked at the others. 'Well, we could do with your suggestions. I may say that young Palfreyman, when I spoke with him last night, was not disposed to insist on a public apology.'

'It's not up to him, is it?' Lightbody demurred, unconsciously echoing the President's earlier words. 'And if Frank won't play alongside Palfreyman, the whole business of the apology is irrelevant anyway.'

'I'm thinking aloud,' Peter Latimer said. 'We could always let Dick go at the end of the season.'

'Bad idea,' Lightbody said, sharply and dismissively. 'It'd be seen at best as vindictive towards a young cricketer who'd made a bad mistake. If the story got out, and it'll get out, it'll look as if we believe Palfreyman's guilty and we could never prove it. We might walk straight into an action for wrongful dismissal.'

'I doubt that, *but* I don't like the notion.' Sir Anthony's voice ran slightly counter to his words. 'We're not dismissing anybody. And we're not, dammit, we're sitting here turning somersaults, if you know what I mean, to keep

Frank on the playing staff. The truth is that he is making himself unavailable for selection.'

Latimer brought his lips tightly together. 'He's absolutely genuine in his belief that the other fellow did him down.'

'He could be absolutely sincere and totally mistaken.'

'I agree, Ken, but the Testimonial worries me. Here's Frank, willing to pass up twenty thousand pounds, and he's never been noted as a prodigal type. He's near, close, miserable, so the dressing-room will tell you. Yet, he'll put his Testimonial at risk.'

'I may be wrong,' the chairman said in the tones of a man who knows his opinion is unassailable, 'but I thought the essence of this club was that a committee, with specified powers, was elected from the ranks of the members. The committee may delegate certain functions to sub-committees, such as ourselves, and we are responsible to the executive committee, and through them to the members, for the discharge of those functions. I am right in thinking that?'

'Perfectly right, Sir Anthony.'

'I am further right, then, in thinking that a player is an employee of the club and, no matter how gifted, has no say in the composition of the side, except, of course,' — he nodded to Peter — 'in the case of the captain.' No one disagreed. 'Well, that's the nub of it.'

'Player power,' Lightbody murmured.

'I prefer to call it the democratic process. We haven't a hope in hell of proving Palfreyman did what he's accused of by Applegarth.'

'So, the original finding has to stand?'

'You know it has, Peter. I feel as badly about it as you do, I've been here longer, I've seen more hard times. Frank carried us through at least three seasons early in his career when we hadn't another batsman worthy of the name.'

'Perhaps with a little more time . . .' Lightbody felt bound to grasp anything that floated.

Sir Anthony Coverdale, urbane in his daily round, could be immovable when exercising his office.

'We don't have time. We agreed to release a statement today. The fine's stiff, I grant you, but no one could say that our decision is unreasonable.'

'You asked for our suggestions, Sir Anthony.'

'I did, Peter. I hope I'll always be open to them.'

'I think I see a way whereby we can make our statement and still gain a little time.'

'Let's have it then.'

'Let's assume that when we have Frank back in a couple of minutes from now, he still stands fast on the two points, that is, he won't apologise to Richard or play alongside him. I don't think we'd need to do anything too drastic immediately.'

'I don't follow you,' the President frowned and, clearly, Ken Lightbody did not either.

'We can leave him out of the Worcester match.'

'And how do you propose to explain that away?'

'In the interests of long-term team-building. It'll be the last game of the current championship and we can't win that. So, we bring in a couple of youngsters, to give them a run.'

'It might work.' Ken Lightbody's grunt conveyed qualified support. 'I'd like to think there was some way of keeping the old basket here.' He appeared suddenly struck by something. 'What happens to the Testimonial if he won't see sense?'

'It lapses. What else?' Latimer's tone was surprised.

'We could,' Sir Anthony said, 'bring young Rupert

Delaval's benefit forward by a year.'

'That's a non-starter,' Lightbody said thoughtfully. 'We operate benefits on the calendar year, and it takes at least a good six months to get a proper organising committee together. It would be most unfair to the lad. Besides, he's off to Antigua week after next. We couldn't chop and change like that.'

'What about Eric's notion, a benefit year for the club?'

'We're not supposed to know about that yet, Peter. I wonder, by the way, if our excellent treasurer has researched that one thoroughly enough.'

'How do you mean, Sir Anthony?'

'Well, an uncle of mine took the case which established the laws on cricketers' benefits, way back. They were untaxed, unlike the poor soccer chaps, because the benefit was held to be not a contractual payment but a token of esteem to the player concerned.'

'You're excelling yourself, Sir Anthony,' Ken Lightbody said ironically. 'Where's the difficulty?'

'I just wonder if the Inland Revenue Commissioners will go along with us presenting a token of our esteem for ourselves to ourselves.' He held up a hand. 'I speak in jest — no doubt Eric has explored every contingency and foreseen every pitfall. Anyway, I've let you sidetrack me. If Applegarth has thought better of things, the question doesn't arise.'

Applegarth hadn't. On the third trying of him, he gave not the slightest sign of any disposition to budge. It was with genuine regret that Sir Anthony spoke.

'I feel that we as a club have gone as far as we could be expected to go. It would not, I feel, be dignified for us to attempt to persuade you any further.' His voice assumed an official, dispassionate tone for the conveyance of information. 'Accordingly, it is our finding that a fine of four hundred pounds be imposed upon you arising from the incident between yourself and Richard Palfreyman near the end of the match against Glamorgan. An apology in a form agreed to be appropriate will be made by you to Richard Palfreyman for your part in the said incident. You are severely censured and warned as to your future conduct while a player with this County. Finally, I shall be seeking the agreement of the cricket committee that in the interests of long-term team-building, you should be omitted from the side to play Worcestershire at Worcester in the last championship match of the season, but without prejudice to your future here.'

'Is that all, Sir Anthony?'

'That's all, except to say that even at this very late stage I would be delighted — I know I speak for all three of us — if the matter can be amicably resolved. It has been deeply unfortunate.'

'I do appreciate that it's a job that you gentlemen would rather have been spared. I see the difficulty you find yourselves in. I hope you'll understand at least partly why I can't do as you ask.'

'We will be issuing a statement to the Press in the form that I read to you.'

'The reporters'll be round me like flies round the honeypot, five minutes afterwards.'

'What'll you tell them, Frank?'

Applegarth looked at his skipper as if he were meeting him for the first time.

'That I think the fine was fair and that I'll be happy to pay it.' A twist of a smile appeared. 'Maybe not "happy" to pay it, that wouldn't carry conviction coming from old Frank Applegarth. I'll tell them I won't apologise and that I won't play with him again.'

'Why not simply say you just won't apologise?'

'It's my decision, Ken, I'll handle it my way.'

'Will you tell the Press why?'

'I don't think so.'

'To justify your actions?'

'I don't feel the need to justify them. I know why I won't.
So does Alice. So do you. The others don't matter. If anyone blabs, it'll not be me. Can I go now?'

Sir Anthony nodded.

'See you, Frank,' his captain said automatically.

The door closed. Sir Anthony signed to Peter. 'Better
fetch the reporters in, Peter. I'll read the statement; it's clear
from the phone calls we made last night that it reflects the
general feeling of the membership. I propose that beyond
that, we say nothing. No questions or points of information
at this stage. If they want any more, they'll have to ferret.'

Peter was out and back, accompanied, in a few strides.
The reporters clustered around the table — there were only
five of them but they filled the microscopic room to burst-
ing. Sir Anthony took a sheet of paper in his hands.

'Good morning, gentlemen. On behalf of the County, I
am authorised to read the following statement to you . . .'

CHAPTER 20

The News Gets Out

By the Thursday morning, it was apparent that the Westercote Festival was heading for a wash-out. There was the
gloomy consolation that if, for the second day in succession, absolutely no play was possible, then there was the
chance of a one-innings match on the last day, with a very
probable result. To be truthful, it was not too much of a
consolation.

In the meantime, one could spend the morning in reading of *l'affaire* Applegarth as seen by the newspapers, each
of which had its individual viewpoint and even more individual syntax. The *Telegraph,* in a thought piece from its
cricket correspondent, came down, as was to be expected,
on the side of sempiternal values.

> In fining heavily their most accomplished
> batsman, the County has struck a blow for
> civilised standards of conduct in the first-
> class game. It is a habit of cricket-writers
> (we include ourselves among them) to con-
> vey the impression that cricket in the
> Golden Age was played only by those

possessing a moral rectitude equivalent to that of St Francis of Assisi. Patently, this was not so. We daresay there must have been occasions when the Great Doctor and Arthur (Shrewsbury) were at odds.

This recent incident is the more unseemly in that one of the principals involved, Frank Applegarth, could hitherto have served as the very model of the modern professional cricketer. Indeed, for many seasons, and at a time when the County were much weaker than, happily, they are now, Applegarth exhibited skill and application to a degree which used to be considered the unique hallmark of the great Yorkshire sides under Hawke and Sellars.

It is not difficult to empathise with the England batsman in his chagrin. Consider a championship to hand for the first time, and a batting record of long standing there for the taking, both to be snatched away by a moment's folly. Frank Applegarth, however, has surely been in the first-class game long enough to realise that there, if anywhere, lurk Triumph and Disaster, those twin imposters of Kipling. He will doubtless even now be regretting his precipitate response to what was at worst a major misjudgment by a young colleague.

The decision to omit him for the match against Worcestershire is to be applauded as a statesmanlike attempt by officials to allow feelings to simmer down. It is true

195

that in not selecting him, the committee has effectively ensured that O.J.T. Manderley's eight centuries in a season will not be surpassed yet awhile. The lesson to be drawn from the whole business, however, is surely that both the pursuit of individual records, and the adulation accorded to those who establish them, are grievously overdone in modern cricket. It is a team game, and we do well to remind ourselves of this great and unalterable truth. It is very much to be hoped that by next season Applegarth will exert in the County dressing-room that beneficent influence which his skill and service in the first-class game uniquely qualify him to impart.

Applegarth laid the *Telegraph* down almost as if the article had referred to someone else entirely. Sir Anthony could have written that article, he thought, but in the thought there was no bitterness. He liked the *Telegraph*, although some of their chaps never used a two-syllable word if a four-syllable one was to hand. Still, although they could be a bit scathing at times, a couple of terms in the Oxford University side didn't teach you it all, and there *were* such things as pitches on which the ball didn't come on to the bat, he liked the sonorous roll of their reporting.

Might as well see what the rest were saying, he thought, noting from the forecast in the *Telegraph* that Lord's too looked like being a wash-out today. If anyone could stop it raining there, John Michael probably could. His mind veered off from the thought of rain to medicine men. In his earliest days he had played against a Somerset captain who'd been born in a Red Indian reservation. He was certain of it, but damned if the name would come. He picked up the *Orb* with its strident headline.

England Bat Fined and Dropped
"Slugger" Applegarth's 400 Quid Left Hook
by Norman Stapler
Your Man in the Know

The stuffy old-school-tie men who run our national game have done it again. Frank Applegarth, for so long lynchpin of the County, has been fined £400 and left out of the side for the last match of the season.

Years of service have gone for nothing. A piffling dressing-room skirmish, which would have gone unnoticed at Highbury or White Hart Lane, has led to a savage fine. Perhaps it's hard for the committee to grasp how severe the fine is since none of them ever required to play the game for money.

So Applegarth and young Dick Palfreyman, new to the County side, had a difference of opinion. So what? From the schemozzle it's caused, you'd almost think it had been deliberate. In the name of Mr Average Cricket Lover I say to the County executive Think Again! It is not too late. Reinstate Applegarth for the match at Worcester. We all want to see him smash Ossie Manderley's record which has stood since the days of cream teas and the Charleston.

There was much more in similar vein. Frank tossed the paper aside, glancing at his watch. As he did so a car horn sounded at the gate. He went to the window and waved to

197

Rupert Delaval that he would be out in a few minutes. He dashed round the kitchen, throwing socks and shirts into a canvas holdall.

'Thanks for driving out, Rupert,' he said after belting himself in. 'It's a real swine having the car in for servicing.'

'Pleasure, man,' Rupert drawled. Without taking his eyes off the road he added, 'Seen the papers this morning?'

'Some of them.'

'What are you aiming to do?'

'Pay the fine.'

'I hear they want you to apologise, Frank.'

'You hear right, sunshine.'

'Will you?'

'No.'

They swished wetly through Nether Locking, Rupert moving the windscreen wiper up a notch.

'Would it make any difference, Frank, if I asked you to consider apologising?'

'No, Rupert, it wouldn't.'

'I know a little bit about biting the tongue, turning the other cheek. When I came over at first I had to take all kinds of crap. It was a great temptation to lash out, to banjo the people who were baiting me. Only, I knew that's exactly what they were wanting me to do.' The black face was stern in remembrance.

'Sure. I can only guess a little at what it was like. But you didn't, even then, apologise for your bloody existence, you had a proper sense of pride.'

'I'd never have lasted here but for you and Alice.'

Applegarth, head shaking, demurred. 'You'd have made it, sunshine, and I'll tell you why. Because you were a good enough cricketer to have made it, that's why. If I helped you, I'm very glad, but first and foremost it was

198

because you were a cricketer, not that you were a black Antiguan cricketer.'

'You believe Richard Palfreyman ran you out deliberately?'

'Yes, I do. I heard him tell me.'

'Even if he had it in for you, why the hell would he want to tell you, to say anything about it?'

'If he had said nothing, it might have been an accident. He wanted me to know.'

'What about being left out for the Worcester game?'

His passenger shrugged. 'They pick the team.'

'You'd still a chance of the ninth century, Frank.'

'In theory, yes, but it's hard to gear yourself up after a disappointment like Tuesday's. It's a long way even to fifty in the county game, and that's only half-way. I think O.J.T. Manderley's record' — he dwelt ironically on the initials — 'is pretty safe. I don't see myself turning out for the County again.'

'What could persuade you?'

'If they gave Palfreyman the bullet. They'll not do that, in fairness they can't do that on a my-word-against-his-basis.'

'I reckon you would have gone to India this winter.'

'I reckon you've got a very fertile imagination, young Rupert,' Applegarth said, but he was pleased and touched nevertheless.

'You've been watched by the selectors, you know that?'

'Don Rydings, Tuesday,' Frank said tonelessly. 'I didn't notice him but the gateman did. I did a quick check of those playing in the match and reckoned it had to be me he was here for.'

Rupert's grin at this piece of objectivity was spotted.

'Well, it had to be, Rupert, hadn't it? You and Ezra

aren't eligible and no-one else is good enough. Anyway it's up the spout now, they won't take players in dispute with their club.'

Rupert's tone was anxious. 'If you don't straighten things out with the boss men, Frank, what then?'

'I'll try for another county. I think there are a couple of possibilities further north. Derbyshire certainly, Notts perhaps. Maybe even Lancashire.'

'It's a different world up there, man.'

'Not all that different. You forget I'm a Lincolnshire man, that's only a kick in the arse from Trent Bridge.'

'What does Alice say?'

'She believes me. She'll do whatever I think is best.'

'Would they be needing a bowler too, by any chance?'

'That's enough!' said Applegarth, an angry lash to his voice. 'You've a benefit coming year after next, you'll have Tilly to consider from now on. No heroic gestures, if you don't mind. Stop at the Post Office for a minute, will you, I've some stamps to get.'

In the beer tent, dressed in what seemed like the leavings of a War Department sale — all anoraks and combat jackets and jungle hats — Alan the poet, Ian from the Inland Revenue, his son Jim, and Stephen McKendrick were engaged in selection of a different sort, an all time Fat Man's XI to play Mars. Alan was inscribing the names in a book.

'W.G. for starters.' McKendrick said.

'And Warwick Armstrong?'

'Definitely Warwick Armstrong,' the Scot nodded approvingly. 'Nice one, Ian.'

'David Shepherd of Gloucester?' This from Ian.

'The bucolic Shepherd,' murmured Alan, the inscriber of the roll.

'I see a snag,' Jim chipped in. 'We're almost bound to be short of bowlers.'

'How about Ian Botham?'

'I don't know about that, Alan. Is Botham a genuine fat man?'

'At times he seems a very genuine fat man.'

'Okay, shove him down, Alan. We can always drop him if he loses form, I mean weight.'

'We'll need a wicket-keeper,' pointed out McKendrick.

Alan was already registering a name. 'We need look no further than our own, our very own, Bernie Masterton.'

'What about Imti?'

'Great, Stephen. Intikhab Alam, world-class leg spinner of aldermanic proportions. The Martians don't stand a chance.'

'Let's give them a chance. I nominate the Maharajah of Vizianagram.'

'Who the hell's he?'

'Captained the All-India side in 1936. I'm appalled at the gaps in your knowledge, young Jim. We shall have to consider seriously whether you are a fit and proper person to be admitted to our counsels.'

'Sorry, Alan.'

'Apology noted and accepted.'

Dick Tyldesley of Lancashire, Phil Meade of Hampshire, Bishan Bedi in his latter years, and Colin Milburn, completed a powerful if unbalanced side. Twelfth man duties were split between Ken Higgs and Eddie Hemmings, although here the selectors were careful to point out that they were looking at potential.

Their deliberations were finished on the stroke of noon, coinciding with the announcement that play had been officially abandoned for the day. The start of the Test Match at

Edgbaston had been delayed, although there was some hope here, so for the next half hour or so, the specialists in rotundity sipped lukewarm beer and watched TV highlights from the 1975 World Cup Final at Lord's.

Palfreyman meanwhile had taken advantage of the early call-off to go round to the Brunel to collect Jenny, who was going back up to London. It was just as well perhaps to be out of Applegarth's way, although with the exception of Delaval, he could detect absolutely no change in the attitude of his team-mates towards him.

He strolled through the lobby of the hotel towards the lift and pressed the button. Nothing happened, and after some time it was evident that the lift was stopped semi-perma nently on the second floor, and that its stablemate was officially out of action and had the printed card to prove it. Impatiently Palfreyman set off to climb the stairs; he felt both damp and overheated and his face was still unsightly.

On the second floor he saw the reason for the non-arrival of his lift. It was crammed with television sets which were being put in as replacements for the older models in the rooms which looked out to the back. Two members of the hotel staff, both men, were manoeuvring the sets from the lift along the corridors to their destined rooms. Palfreyman was about to take the third flight at a run when, as from nowhere, the name of Applegarth burst from their conversation. He stood round the corner on the second stair of the third flight, well within earshot.

'Bloody shame,' came the voice, 'fining him that amount of money and dropping him. He's carried that bunch of deadbeats for years.'

The older voice that responded to this was unreceptive. 'He can afford it. That'll be the day when you and I make enough to be fined that kind of money. Besides, who's to say he didn't deserve it anyway?'

'It was the other bloke's fault, you know, the young chap.'

Palfreyman's stab of annoyance at his own anonymity was engulfed in the shock of the senior man's next words.

'If you ask me, he was probably knackered, the randy old bastard. He was in here last Friday night, you know.'

'Sure. At the Mayor's Reception.'

'Sure,' came the derisive drawl. 'And at least for four hours after that.'

'How do you know, Len?'

'Because I was standing in for night porter for Donald, wasn't I? Your Mr Applegarth was up there on the third floor, boffing that young bit of stuff from London. Half his luck, chance'd be a fine thing, wouldn't mind an hour screwing her.'

'Get on. He was probably seeing one of the committee.'

'Till four in the morning? That's when he left. Riordan knows about it, he fairly choked me off when I mentioned it to him, stuck-up sod. C'mon, Joe, give us a hand with this bastard.' Scraping and bumping noises indicated that a set was being dragged from the lift and lugged along the corridor. The discontented, whining voice receded.

Palfreyman stood transfixed on the staircase. Despite strenuous attempts at control, he was aware of his colour coming and going. Did Applegarth think that he knew? That was to assume that the hotel porter had spoken the truth. Did Applegarth, on that assumption, therefore think that this was the motivation for the run-out? He hadn't mentioned it in the scuffle and after, but what a potent weapon of ridicule was available to the senior man if he chose to use it. Palfreyman writhed at the thought, then comforted himself.

For, of course, Applegarth would not use it, dare not use it, because of Alice. Indeed it was perhaps a lever that had been placed in his own hands. In the meantime, there was one way to find out, and that was to confront Jenny with the situation. Perhaps she had slept with Applegarth, perhaps not, but he knew her well enough to be convinced that she would not lie in the face of a direct question. He climbed the remaining stairs at no great pace, and by the time he knocked on the door of Room 327 his complexion was normal and his face expressionless.

CHAPTER 21

Richard and Jenny

Seated in the hotel room's only chair, Richard Palfreyman watched from a distance as Jenny, with a few passes of the hands, neatly transferred a mound of toiletries, dresses, tops, underwear and shoes to the confines of a medium-sized suitcase. As she did so she spoke to him over her shoulder.

'It'll be good to get a lift to the station. I'd almost settled for a taxi.'

'After the call-off there wasn't much point in hanging round the ground. You can play only so much solo.'

'I'm glad I just manage to edge out the card school,' Jenny said brightly, exerting considerable downward pressure on the lid of her suitcase. She turned towards him and her eyes narrowed at the tautness of his face.

'More trouble with Frank Applegarth?'

'No. I hardly saw him this morning. There's a well-orchestrated plot to keep us out of each other's way.'

'Then, why so gloomy? Unless of course it's that you're overcome by grief at my imminent departure.'

He held up a hand defensively. 'Not today, Jenny, I'm not in the humour for the clever stuff.'

'I can see that. What's put you out of sorts, Richard? You can tell poor Jenny.'

'I'm not sure I can.'

'But you're going to,' the girl said with a flash of insight. She came over to kneel beside him and noted the slight involuntary retraction. In a changed tone she said slowly. 'What's the matter, Richard?'

There was no further hesitation. In a leaden voice he recounted to her what he had heard on the stairs, toning down the references to the older porter's sexual ambitions and desires.

'I felt like the classic fool. I wanted to fill the swine in, but I couldn't see what that would achieve. I thought of reporting him to the manager, but then I thought that wouldn't be very sensible either, it would perhaps just spread the rumour.'

Jenny looked at him sitting hunched in the chair, gazing beyond her, and for an instant her face was sorrowful.

'Why don't you ask me right out, Richard? It's what you're desperate to do.'

'Ask you what?'

'If Frank Applegarth was in this room last Friday night, if we went to bed together.'

'Well, did you?' in a dry voice.

'Yes, Richard. He was, and we did.'

He breathed heavily, nodded. 'May I ask why?'

'I have no reason that you would begin to understand or accept. How can one accept the unacceptable? If I tried to explain it would probably be even more hurtful than the event.'

'Try.'

'We went to the disco after the Mayor's Reception. We danced together quite a lot. Frank dances very well.' She got up and moved across the room, looking out the window to the seafront. Quietly she went on. 'For a couple of hours he seemed the most attractive man on God's earth.' She laughed harshly. 'Maybe women don't think with their brains.'

'I see.'

'I wonder if you do when I don't see at all clearly myself. I was sorry for it, desperately sorry, before he had closed the door.'

'I'm sorry he was such a disappointment to you.'

Jenny started to speak, then checked. Outside, the straining flag of the hotel tugged at the flagstaff with a dull, metallic chink in the rising wind. Within the room the silence was intense, the two figures immobile.

'Thank you for telling me,' Palfreyman finally said.

'I don't want to add lying to my delinquencies.'

'No, of course not. It's an unusual word for it, delinquency.'

'You've been hurt quite badly.'

'A lesson learned, I think. And better now than at some later time.' His voice — would-be dismissive — lacked total conviction, there was too obvious an attempt to shrug off as trifling something that patently was not.

'What does that mean, Richard?'

'It means I'm glad I found out now. I've seen other players who've had it on their mind when we've been out on the road. "What's the wife doing back home, and who's she doing it with?" It's not an edifying spectacle.' His attempt at quiet control splintered and he burst out in a furious, low tone, 'A couple of drinks, a couple of dances, and he was up here. Christ! It doesn't take much for you to open your legs!'

Jenny looked at him with mild regret, as yet unangered. 'You could well be right, Richard. A couple of nights hard talking at Reading that weekend. That's all it took, wasn't it?'

'To do it with that bastard, of all people!'

When Jenny spoke again her voice was colder, sharper. 'It doesn't excuse my actions one iota, Richard, but you'd have betrayed *me* at the drop of a hat — well, not a hat exactly.'

'How can you say that?'

'Because it's true. To you I'm a good chum, a good lay, someone to tow around and show off, someone who'll go down well with the County committee. I've never seriously flattered myself that I'm anything more.'

She plunged into her handbag for cigarette and lighter and lit up, fingers steady. 'You are a dear, naive soul in some ways, Richard. You can only have sex because there are liberated girls. And, if girls are liberated, you must cease to be surprised when once in a while one of them acts like me. Once in a very long while. I don't propose to make a habit of it.'

'Applegarth would expect you to turn pro if you wanted to do that,' Palfreyman said savagely.

Jenny's stricken look and stung retort were testimony to the accuracy of his thrust.

'If I ever turn pro, as you put it, I'll expect to be able to use you as a referee. You'd be a very valuable endorsement.'

There was another long silence, broken by Jenny. 'You could do the really difficult thing, Richard, you could forgive me. I think I could forgive you if our positions had been reversed.' She sounded almost timid.

Palfreyman made no direct answer to her.

'Can you credit it, that randy little bastard, married with

a couple of kids, and screwing all round him?'

'It happens, Richard.'

'It happens because pushovers like you let it happen. You're the one who doesn't touch married men, remember?'

'I remember. I should have remembered last Friday, and now I'm liable not to forget in a very long while. When you're a married man, Richard, can you tell me absolutely that you'll never lay hands on another woman?'

'I think I could safely say that, yes.'

'No-one can safely say anything like that, Richard. The best one can ever do is try very hard.'

'I'll guarantee to try harder than you, or that little philandering bastard. I wonder if his wife knows?'

'I don't think so. I have dreadful moments when I think what I've done to her, it is a great wrong. Frank will hardly tell her and nobody else knows.'

'The removal men, have you forgotten about them? And anybody who passed along the bloody second floor corridor a few minutes ago.' In an embittered, malevolent tone he mused, 'Someone ought to tell Alice Applegarth what her husband's like.'

'Just make sure it isn't you, Richard, that's all.'

'She's entitled to know what a groping, lecherous sod she's drawn out the hat.'

Jenny went into the bathroom, ran the cold tap, and sipped a glass of water before coming back into the room.

'We're both saying vicious, hurtful things. You've every right to be shocked at me, angry with me, disgusted with me. There's the slight shrinking from polluted flesh, I see. Maybe we're all more Victorian than we think. But I warn you, don't say anything to Alice.'

'Are you as scared as all that?'

'Not in the sense that you mean. I just wouldn't want a marriage to split up because for an hour I behaved like an alley-cat. Besides, you're not in the least concerned with helping Alice. "She's entitled to know." That's the reason given for every piece of filth in the papers, people are "entitled to know". You haven't the remotest wish to help Alice by telling her, your whole desire is to crucify Frank.'

'You have a very low opinion of me, Jenny.'

'Much higher than the one I have of myself, I promise you, but in the matter of Alice you've got to be prevented.'

'You've no way of stopping me, if I choose to do so.'

'I think I have.' The conviction in her voice made him look sharply at her. 'Oh, not by threatening to walk out of here for ever, or even by actually doing it. I don't over-estimate my importance to you.'

'Then what's the great master-stroke?'

'Simply this. If I suspect that you mention a word of this to Alice, or even that you are instrumental in ensuring that she gets to know, I shall at once tell the committee that I have reason to believe that you ran out Frank Applegarth deliberately.'

'That's an outrageous suggestion even for your recent form.'

'It's surprising how the notion's got about. Mrs Masterton thoughtfully showed me that fellow Stapler's article this morning. There are all sorts of rumours flying about.'

'And that's exactly what they are. Rumours.'

'I'm sure they are. Unfounded. Unprovable. So long, that is, as you leave Alice alone, and I don't have to go to the committee.'

'The committee would never believe you.'

'They might well do if I told them that you had told me.'

Palfreyman shook his head with a stimulated wryness but Jenny cut in on him. 'Sir Anthony will think in that situation, "Why should she lie?" He has me figured as your nice young lady, and if one or two of his less charitable chums try to tag me as an up-market camp-follower, the question still remains, why should I lie? You'd be finished with the County, Richard, and well you know it. You'd be out, and that'd matter to you much more than I do. Frank Applegarth's punches, my testimony, the newspaperman's insinuations. Out or in?'

Palfreyman tapped his left palm with his right fist. 'Out.' He began to feel overmatched.

'Whereas, if they don't *know*, and they don't, they'll keep you on next season. You did well in the first innings, and they'll hardly fire you for an honest mistake. Will they keep you on?'

His sullen, joyless tone was in contrast with his news. 'Almost certainly. Charlie Cullis is retiring at the end of the season and they'll maybe give me a shot at opening. If Applegarth goes,' he lingered on the name like an obscenity, 'there are two batting places vacant.'

Jenny looked at her watch. 'I have to watch my time.' She came towards him. 'I levelled with you, Richard, much good may it do me. I believed, silly me, all that equal partnership stuff. Seems the agony aunts don't live in the real world. Was yours an honest mistake?'

'I'm surprised you can ask me that.'

'I'm surprised too,' Jenny said thoughtfully. 'I'll take your word, of course, though you certainly hate him enough to have done it. Why do you dislike him so intensely? And don't say it has anything remotely to do with last Friday night.'

'It might just have done, had you seen fit to inform me

211

about last Friday night. But you're right, I dislike him for other reasons. I dislike him because he's mean with money, mean-spirited. You can't give people a hard time just because you happen to be extremely proficient at a game. It's the only bloody thing he does better than I.'

'You wouldn't expect me to comment on that,' said Jenny, then with an immediate burst of contrition, 'Forget I said that. It was cheap and nasty.'

'Right on both counts.'

Jenny spoke in genuine self-accusation. 'Eight months ago I was an infinitely nicer person. But Richard, this vendetta against Frank, there's something almost feminine about it, how can you drive him out?'

'How can *you* talk such nonsense? His going or staying is not in my hands. The committee wanted him to make a public apology to me and I let them know I wouldn't insist on it. Since he in turn has let them know that he won't play in any side of which I'm part, he's effectively dealing himself out of consideration.' In a voice dripping with sarcasm he said, 'It's always possible, of course, that I've forgotten what actually happened. Perhaps I went for the irresistible Applegarth.'

Jenny lifted her handbag and case. 'It's time I moved, or I'll miss the train.' She hesitated. 'Maybe the taxi would be the better idea after all.'

'Don't be stupid. I'll have you there in five minutes. Give me the case and don't be a damned fool.'

'Let me check to see I haven't forgotten anything.' She picked up his look and said, wearily, 'Well, anything else.'

The lift soared up, swift, noiseless, to meet them.

In the car they made arrangements to meet again. 'I'll come up to London on Sunday. We've the day off, we've already played Worcestershire in the John Player League.'

'Give me a couple of days or so, Richard. I've a busy day on Sunday getting ready to go back to work. I need a day for hair-washing and such-like.'

'Whatever you say. Let's see, Monday and Tuesday we've the Worcester game, Wednesday we're back at the County ground for a single-wicket competition, Viv Richards, Ian Botham, Clive Lloyd, Zaheer Abbas, a few others. We peasants are needed as cannon-fodder in the field. The sponsors are a local building society, there'll be some worthwhile contacts there.'

'You've got as far as Wednesday.'

'I'll come up on Thursday. You'll be at work, naturally.'

'Naturally.'

'Suppose we were to say the Basil Astoria at six o'clock?'

'Half-past is better. We try to clear the weekend mail on Thursdays.'

'All right. We can have a couple of drinks and see where we are.'

He deftly manoeuvred the car into a three-quarter space in the station car park and helped Jenny to wriggle out. They had four minutes in hand and he bought a platform ticket. He made a great display of looking down the line for the imminent train.

'Richard?'

'Uhuh?'

'You're really set on succeeding as a cricketer?'

'Yes. I will. Opening will suit me, I've got the temperament for grafting away. If you read *Wisden*, the most unlikely people make a go of it as openers, some of them live to make their thousand runs in the season.'

'Isn't it a job for the very best batsmen?'

'Thanks a lot. Yes and no. A great many of the best batsmen are scared stiff of opening, it's purely a mental thing. It's my best chance of making it, I know that.'

'What about the winter?'

'I'm still hopeful. There's always a club in Ozzie or South Africa who've been let down and need someone in a hurry. I'll try to get a couple of good scores at Worcester, that would help a little.'

'And if nothing comes of it?'

'Peter Latimer has the scouts out for me as Plan B. I might get a term's teaching somewhere.'

They walked the length of the platform past the floral arrangements and the enormous, flattering poster of Westercote, which would hardly convince its own citizens, who knew better.

'Here she comes. Got everything? Ticket?'

Jenny nodded. 'Thank you for having me down.'

'Thank you for coming.'

The formal phrases fell heavily.

'Where do we go now, Richard?'

He carried her case on to the train, putting it on the rack above a pleasant, motherly soul. Then he regained the platform and Jenny pushed down the window of the corridor door.

'We'll take it from Thursday,' he said. 'There's a lot to say yet.'

She took his hand as the train moved off slowly. Her primrose-coloured raincoat made a vivid splash of colour against the wet gloom, and she waved vigorously as the train went into a steep left-hand curve. For as long as Jenny was in vision Palfreyman remained standing on the platform, but he did not wave.

CHAPTER 22

Close of Play

The Warwickshire match did not in the end quite attain the melancholy status of a wash-out. It was possible to begin play under a watery sun at eleven o'clock and the visiting side, on winning the toss, had neither hesitation nor compunction in asking the County to bat. In forty-three uneventful minutes they progressed to twenty-seven for the loss of Charlie Cullis's wicket, he on his last-ever home appearance, being trapped in front by Bob Willis for five. Just before a quarter-to twelve clouds again banked up, the rain fell in sullen streams, and the already sodden ground could take no more. The players scampered from the field gleefully, relieved to have escaped from the non-match. Nobody had starred, nobody had been damaged, if one excepted Charlie Cullis, who would have wished to register a more positive farewell.

In the home dressing-room there was a great throwing around of gloves, bats and pads as cricket-bags were packed in the light-hearted atmosphere that an unexpected day off always brought. Negotiations were in progress regarding transport for the Worcester match — who would drive, what cars should be taken. Palfreyman, straightening up over his bag, made an offer to Rupert.

'Want to come up in my car, Rupert? Seems pointless to take two where one'll do.'

'No, thanks. I've made arrangements.'

'Fine. Whatever you say.'

'You could give me a lift, Richard,' Latimer said somewhat too quickly. 'It'd be nice not to have to drive and to be able to devote my mind to weighty tactical decisions.'

Palfreyman's was a manifest pleasure. 'Done, Peter. I'll pick you up — when shall we say, eight o'clock?'

'Better make it seven-thirty. Has Sir Anthony spoken to you about opening?'

Sir Anthony had, under the impression that it was his idea, although in various fragments of conversation Palfreyman had assiduously and obliquely planted the notion.

'Charlie Cullis is giving up, as you know, Richard, and we'll need an opener. Would you consider having a run at it?'

'It's a pretty specialised thing, opening.' Palfreyman had allowed his voice to register a becoming doubt. 'I'm not sure you'd find me up to it.'

'Nonsense, I'm convinced you've the temperament for it, and that's more than half the battle. You're not exactly the most dashing stroke player we've ever had, but that's not necessarily a fault in an opener. In any case, you'd be opening with Jimmy Briers, and he gets on with it. A dasher and an anchor man, that's no bad recipe for an opening pair. How about it?'

'I'll be happy to play anywhere that the committee thinks might benefit the side, Sir Anthony.' A thought appeared to strike him. 'I take it the skipper has no objection?'

'On the contrary, he was delighted at my suggestion. By the way, when I said have a run at it, I meant exactly that. I think we'd like you to feel that, barring accidents, the number one spot was yours for next May and June. That'd give you a fair chance to settle down, see how you fancy the job and how it fancies you.'

'It'd be the number two spot surely? Jimmy's a lot senior to me.'

'Nothing or nobody will induce Jimmy Briers to take first strike. He's resisted all offers and suggestions for fifteen years, I don't see him undergoing a sea change now.' The speaker straightened his I Zingari tie, a fruitless labour given the floppiness of his collar. 'Good, we've settled that. Might as well start at Worcester, don't you think?'

'Isn't it a bit sudden?'

'No, I think not. Charlie Cullis knows it's on the cards and we won't hold failure against you, Richard. Not even, God forbid, a king pair.'

Rupert Delaval spoke to Applegarth as the latter shrugged his way into a green blazer.

'What time will I pick you up tomorrow?'

'No need.'

'But your car's still off the road?'

'True, oh king! However, since I'm not playing, the question doesn't arise, remember?'

'I know that. I thought you'd maybe come along to watch.'

Applegarth looked at him narrowly. 'Not a good idea. I don't much like watching cricket, I really don't. I don't want to go up there and be thought to gloat if our mutual friend fails, and I'm far from being Christian enough to

217

rejoice if he comes off.'

'Charlie told me he's being tried as an opener.'

'He can try.'

Rupert scowled, his face thoughtful. 'I could just see him being an opener, Frank. I don't like the conniving bastard but he's dogged.'

'Sure he is. He'll stick around for an hour and a half for a dogged ten. It's not enough to be strokeless to be an opener. You need technique and he's never shown me he's got it.'

Rupert decided against pursuing the conversation. Basically he agreed with Applegarth anyway, and in the veteran cricketer's frame of mind, there was little point in further discussion. So he simply said, 'You won't change your mind about Worcester?'

'No. If I needed another reason, I don't want to spend all day tomorrow dodging reporters who'll sympathise with me and try to get me to say something stupid.'

'So how will you spend the day?'

'With the boys. It'll be good for them to realise their dad's not just a fellow on the telly on Sundays. Maybe I'll straighten Richard's grip out. He holds the bat like a saw, it's high time he stopped.'

'What about his brother?'

'Rodney? Better grip, better stance, no power. Richard, oddly enough, has the makings but the Bedsers they're not.' He looked around the dressing-room. 'Well, that's everything. I'm off.'

'See you then, Frank.'

'See you, Rupert. I'll keep up with the scores on the radio. You'll have to be at your best on that track, sunshine. Still, get rid of Glenn Turner, Alan Ormrod and the old man and there's not too much left. Line and length, sunshine, line and length.'

In the beer tent Stephen McKendrick stood in the familiar knot of acquaintances — Alan the poet, Ian the tax-
gatherer, and Jim, who shared his father's obsession for
vegetables to such a degree that he had gone professional.
Each of them was clutching the sovereign specific against
the weather, the fixture-list for the following season.

'Northants and Yorkshire for the two county matches,'
Alan read aloud, 'with Essex in on the Sunday for the JPL.
Not a bad Festival, Stephen? Worth coming down again
from your haggis-infested moors?'

'Not at all bad,' Stephen agreed.

'I've never understood,' Ian said, in his precise, Civil
Service voice, 'why you don't support Yorkshire, Stephen,
living where you do.'

'That's why you're a money-grubbing leech,' Alan told
him amiably. 'Not a scrap of romance or poetry in you.
What's the tie, Steve?'

McKendrick took a quick look-down at his shirt front
across which fell a dark blue tie with golden umbrellas and
cricket stumps.

'Oh,' he grinned, 'I've always got to check. It's the RSP
tie, rain stopped play. Qualification is three first-class
matches attended and totally washed out.'

'Can you get me one, Stephen?'

'I'll try, but I don't think so, Jim. I bought this years ago
in London in a little tie shop in Villiers Street, near Strand
Tube station. The shop's away long since — come to think
of it, there's no Strand Tube station either.'

Ian drove in on him. 'To more important things. Will
Frank Applegarth be here next season?'

'Of course he will.' Alan had no doubt. 'He's a canny lad,
our Frank. He's not going to throw a benefit and an
England place away for a trivial, stupid punch-up.'

'Was he going to India?' McKendrick wanted to know.

'He must be in with a great shout. He's your real infantryman, Applegarth. When it's India, a couple of the delicate blossoms always call off late in the day. You need the strong forearms and the strong gut.'

'The County couldn't afford to lose him.'

'That's right, Jim,' Ian nodded. 'No doubt people like us said the same thing in Yorkshire beer tents about Close, Illingworth, Johnny Wardle, Jackie Hampshire. But they all went off on their travels just the same.'

'That was *Yorkshire*, Ian.' Alan emphatically made the distinction between the rational and the irrational world.

'I wonder if you're right, Alan,' Stephen McKendrick said thoughtfully. 'You've heard the buzz, that Frank won't play in the same side as young Palfreyman. I don't see how, if it's true, you can let players make that kind of statement. He's not in the side for Worcester.'

'A touch on the bridle, nothing more. I remember reading that when Nelson Eddy wouldn't renew his contract, the film studio had Alan Jones sing a few songs in his hearing to change his mind.'

'And now Alan opens for Glamorgan. There's success for you!'

'Shut up, Jim!'

In amiable bickering, in animated discussion, the next hour passed. Through the tent opening they were able to observe the melancholy process of dismemberment. Already the scaffolding of the stands was being dismantled with heavy metallic clinking. The mayor's tent was the first to be struck, its inhabitants spirited away by the calls of office. The hatches of the mobile County shop were slammed shut, and with much revving of the engine and much grinding of gears it negotiated the narrow gates and

220

set off for winter quarters at the County ground. Behind it at an equally stately pace came the caravan of umpire Charles Dodd which would bump all across southern England until it reached Folkestone. At irregular intervals players' cars took off like hornets. McKendrick told himself it was perfectly understandable, without totally overcoming the layman's wonder that gifted people should actually *want* to leave a county cricket ground.

The reporters had hushed their chattering portables, the scoreboard returned to its initial zeroes. Crippledyke's high season was over. Next week, the well-to-do ladies from the surrounding well-to-do houses would be walking their Sealyhams over the wicket and in a month or so the local hockey club would be doing horrendous things to the outfield.

Two boys, with unnecessary clatter, began to throw the sodden folding chairs from the members' enclosure into a lorry. In the beer tent the crowd was beginning perceptibly to thin out. Joyce Tattersall, while not quite applying the closure, was beginning to emit bat-like signals that departures should not be too long delayed.

'One more then,' Alan said.

They did not linger over the last pint. By being back before two, Ian could save half a day's leave, Jim was chafing over what so much rain might do to the market garden.

'Next year then, and a merry meeting.'

Stephen McKendrick had always been uncomfortable with this phrase, self-conscious about it, but now it seemed quite natural. The four men parted, informally, abruptly, knowing they could take up next year almost without the skip of a heartbeat.

At the gate Stephen paused to look back at the ground before going to his car and noticed he'd been wrong in one particular. They hadn't got around to taking the score off the small scoreboard. Twenty seven for one as the end product of a three-day match, his last if the experts were right. Perfect, God the Supreme Artist. A cliff-hanger would have been too much, a total wash-out a cliché. This score of marvellous futility summed up the infuriation and the enchantment of the three-day game.

He would, when he went back to the Malt Shovel, book in again for the following year. That was his usual pattern, and not to do so would be to invite George's comment and concern. He could confirm on New Year's Day.

An hour or so ago they had heard that Middlesex had got the points they needed for outright victory in the championship. That was right and fitting, the championship should go to the best side, and Middlesex were incontestably that. Middlesex set him thinking of Lord's and that made the connection with Francis Thompson's poem, *At Lord's*, to his mind the only cricket poem, although there was some fine verse. There had been a time when he found the poem cloying, even yet he was not entirely sure of 'O my Hornby and my Barlow long ago!'

In his present situation, however, the poem had inevitably acquired a heightened significance. It was as if Thompson had written for him.

For the field is full of shades as I near the shadowy coast,
And a ghostly batsman plays to the bowling of a ghost,
And I look through my tears on a soundless-clapping host
As the run-stealers flicker to and fro, to and fro:
O my Hornby and my Barlow long ago!

He thrust a hand into his anorak pocket for the car keys and felt his fingers closing over a folded piece of paper. He drew it out — next year's fixture-list. Northants and York-shire with Essex on the Sunday. As he looked at it, he rea-lised that the resignation he thought he had acquired did not exist.

It should have been possible to go out philosophically. There was no great postwar player that he had been denied, Hutton, Compton, Lock, Laker, Harvey, Sobers, Donnelly and a host of others besides — he'd relished them all. He'd seen Pakistan come and South Africa go. He'd watched as the game underwent the chemotherapy of the one-day competitions, and held his breath as Lord's seemed to falter before recognising its responsibilities over the D'Oliveira business. The bar-room brawl between Kerry Packer and the City had been proof of the passionate responses that the game could still evoke, and he had lived to see a fellow-countryman captain the full England side. He had been given, in every sense of the word, a good inn-ings. Yet, however ungrateful it might appear, he knew that he was not remotely prepared to let go. Why should Jim, Alan and Ian be there next year and he not? Doctors had been wrong before, hadn't they? The least that Liz was entitled to was a fight for it, a run for her money. If he could get through the winter, and the spring beyond, he could make next summer.

He felt himself tingle with a wholly irrational energy. It would be good to meet Liz off the train at Temple Meads tonight, to share the affectionate, needling phrases of twenty plus years together as they drove north again. And — just in case! — they would call in at Worcester for a day or so. It would be very interesting to see what kind of a fist young Palfreyman made of it as opening partner to Jim Briers. He transferred the fixture-list carefully to his wallet and turned the key in the ignition.